"Did you really ▓▓▓▓▓ Miss O'Leary?"

"What?" Joan answere▓ ▓▓▓▓▓ daydreamir▓ ▓▓▓▓▓▓ ▓▓▓ ▓▓▓ the gorgeous lawman in a s▓▓ ▓. handcuffs. She started. "Oh! Yes. Yes, I killed him. In a fit of passion."

"Yeah, that's right. Passion." Dan looked her over, then shook his head. "Nope. Don't see it. Not you."

Joan zeroed in on his insult. "You don't think I can be passionate? Not that it's any of your business, but I can be as passionate as the next woman— maybe even more. And don't you forget it."

A husky chuckle preceded his words. "I won't. I'm just glad to know that all that red hair and those green eyes weren't wasted on someone with no fire." Dan dug into his pocket and pulled out some keys. "Stand up, please."

She tensed, breathing shallowly. "Are you cutting me loose?"

Dan shook his head. "No. You've been arrested and charged. Only the D.A. can cut you loose." Pulling the handcuffs off her, Dan asked, "I *can* trust you not to try to escape, can't I?"

Joan looked at him sweetly. "As much as you can any other cold-blooded killer."

Dear Reader,

Runaway brides and runaways seem to be the theme this month in a pair of great romps!

Renee Roszel always writes great comedy about heroes and heroines you really do fall in love with, and *There Goes the Bride* (rather self-explanatory) is no different. It is also the first of a mini marathon of Western-themed romances coming out in the next four months. Cowboys and the women who lasso their hearts. You, too, will fall head over spurs for these love stories!

Cheryl Anne Porter's heroine can think of only one really safe place to hide from the Mafia, and therefore confesses to a crime she didn't commit. The only problem is that no one thinks she's guilty—certainly not the sexy deputy assigned to escort her to jail. The only thing to do is to plan *The Great Escape*.

So take some time to smell the roses (it is May!) and enjoy yourself with two great LOVE & LAUGHTER books.

Malle Vallik

Malle Vallik
Associate Senior Editor

THE GREAT ESCAPE
Cheryl Anne Porter

Harlequin Books

TORONTO • NEW YORK • LONDON
AMSTERDAM • PARIS • SYDNEY • HAMBURG
STOCKHOLM • ATHENS • TOKYO • MILAN
MADRID • WARSAW • BUDAPEST • AUCKLAND

ISBN 0-373-44044-8

THE GREAT ESCAPE

Copyright © 1998 by Cheryl Anne Porter

Printed in U.S.A.

A funny thing happened...

I'm not a good liar, I hate flying, I can't ski and I'm intimidated by policemen, not to mention bears. But I love to tell a good story. So, in *The Great Escape,* what else could I do but put all these elements together? Of course, I desperately needed to do some research (since I generally don't know much about things I avoid). So I pestered very *big* policemen and very *busy* pilots into answering a few questions. It didn't take long before they were threatening to throw me into a cell or out of an airplane if I didn't go away! Now I know how my heroine, Joan, feels. She wasn't the only one who had to make The Great Escape!

—Cheryl Anne Porter

Books by Cheryl Anne Porter

HARLEQUIN LOVE & LAUGHTER
21—A MAN IN DEMAND

To the men in my life—
Paul, Paul III, Nick, TJ, Jimmie and Mark.
Heroes all, and all beloved to me.

1

IT'S KIND OF HARD to scratch your nose when you're hand-cuffed, Joan was forced to conclude as she tried but failed to raise her manacled hands to her face. She sat down with her chain mates as ordered, but immediately turned her head and tried to rub the dastardly tickle against her raised shoulder. Her snorting, sighing and iron-clanking efforts, while easing her itch, suddenly sounded awfully loud to her. But surely she wasn't as—

She peeked. Lots of curious stares were coming her way. Lots. Joan straightened up, relaxed her posture. *Great. That's what I want—freak-show status in a women's prison.* Could she help it, she argued right back, that her every move made her sound like the Ghost of Christmas Past? No, but she needed to look that scary if she hoped to keep body and soul intact.

Conceding that point, Joan cramped her features into a glare meant to convey what-are-you-looking-at-sister. Apparently it did, because the rough women averted their gazes. Joan lowered hers to her lap. Prison coveralls, compliments of Houston's penal system, engulfed her body. Her oh-so-fashionable orange jumpsuit and matching chain accessories didn't matter, she told herself. What did matter was that she was safely in jail. Thank God.

That's how grim things were. Being a criminal was a good thing in her life. As was being charged with Murder One. Not to mention the possibility of death by lethal injection. Great. *Don't even go there, girlfriend. Your nerves are already frayed like split ends. Worry about today, about why you were taken out of your nice cell and marched in a chain gang to the Holding Room.*

Good point. She swept the room with her gaze, wondering where *were* the peeling paint and the dirty floors and the dripping overhead pipes? Didn't these people watch TV? Obviously not, because the large, well-lit room was depressingly clean and…well, about as visually interesting as an air vent. But still, nitpicking her surroundings was better than being sociable with her "Who's Who in Women's Prisons Today" comrades. Especially Big Betty. Big Betty sat next to her. Big Betty *liked* to sit next to her.

And to stare at her. Like now. Feeling the woman's assessing, piggy-eyed gaze riveted on her, Joan attempted to inch away. But the chain that looped her waist—and also attached her to Big Betty's girth—prevented her from doing more than yanking her own chain.

"What're you in for, honey?"

Joan froze. Maybe if she just pretended she hadn't heard her. But her shoulder being bumped forced her to turn to her chain mate. Joan stared at the woman's broad and sweaty frying-pan face. And blinked. Finally, she managed to croak out, "I'm in for murder. I killed someone."

"So that's what murder means." Big Betty snorted out a chuckle. "Who'd you kill—the pet groomer for clipping your poodle too close?" Then she and her bad breath leaned over, got in Joan's face. "You wouldn't kill a rabid dog if it attacked you, doll."

Joan's belly plummeted like a plunging roller coaster. *This is not good.* Hoping Big Betty would leave her alone if Big Betty thought she was crazy, Joan grimaced and snarled, "I ain't nobody's doll, sister. And you're wrong, see? I am guilty. Guilty, I tell ya! I ain't like these cry-baby dames here in the joint, whining about they're innocent. Not me—I whacked him. And whacked him good. He had it coming.''

To Joan's further horror, Big Betty's face lit with admiration. "Hey, I seen that movie, too! I like your style, kid. *And* them Irish good looks of yours. Yep, Big Betty's thinking you're gonna be re-e-al popular in the old cell block." Then she adopted a whispering, conspiratorial air. "You'll need a…friend to look after you. Know what I mean?"

No, no, no rang in Joan's head, but she found herself nodding yes. But only because she did know and feared exactly what Big Betty meant.

"Good," the large woman concluded. "Because I ain't got a cell mate no more. See, Sunny—my last old lady— well, she thought she could mess around on me. But I taught her different. It was a hard lesson, but she had it coming." She shrugged her linesman's shoulders, adding, "Maybe she'll walk again one day. But you? You look sweet. You wouldn't mess around on Big—"

"All right, ladies, pipe down and listen up. Hey, I said shut up."

Joan jerked toward the cavalry-to-the-rescue sound of Sergeant Mackleman's voice. Standing at the room's far entrance, a clipboard clutched in his hand, he called out, "I'm looking for Debutante Number 8-7-6-3-4-1-9. Check your dance cards, ladies, and speak up. I got work to do here."

When no one responded to the guard's repeated call, Joan thought to consult the stenciling above her left breast. 8763419. She gasped, crying out, "Oh, it's me. I'm Joan—I mean 8-7-6-3-4-1-9. Right here, Sergeant Mackleman. Over here!"

Seeing the guard's handlebar mustache droop in a frown

as he searched the orange ocean of seated prisoners, Joan nearly cut herself in half trying to wriggle to her feet. But the ironclad restraint of her waist chains and ankle chains and handcuffs-chained-to-her-waist chains jerked her back. Her rump smacked down onto the hardest chair in the history of civilized sitting.

Grimacing, Joan settled for waggling her hands desperately as she sang out, "Yoo-hoo? Over here. I'm 8-7-6-3-4-1-9. You remember me—from last weekend when I turned myself in?"

To her infinite relief, Joan saw the big guard zero in on her bouncing commotion. He shook his head as he started toward her, already reaching for the ring of keys clipped to his belt. When he stood at the end of her row, he eyed her and muttered, "I should've known. The princess."

Barely able to contain herself, Joan cut her gaze over to Big Betty's sweaty presence and then, when the big guard stood in front of her, turned an imploring expression up to the armed man. "Could I request solitary confinement, please? It's nothing personal against these women. I'm sure they're all very nice. It's just that…well, I know me, and I'm a lousy roommate. I love bread and water. *Hate* sunshine and exercise."

The gruff officer eyed her, shot a look at Big Betty, and then back at Joan. Leaning over her, he lowered his voice to say, "For what it's worth, O'Leary, if you don't start telling the truth, if you stick with your present story, you're sitting next to your future, kiddo. And unlike you, it ain't pretty."

Pursing her lips in defeat, Joan looked away from him to a Crime Doesn't Pay poster tacked up on a far wall. *Oh, sure, now they tell me.* But did Sergeant Mackleman really think she *wanted* to be here? Tell the truth, he said. Yeah, right. The truth, as a famous someone once said, shall set you free. *And thereby get me killed.* Knowing that, she again sought the well-meaning guard's brown eyes. "I'm sticking to my story."

Sergeant Mackleman sighed and straightened up. "Suit yourself." He wrote something on a form attached to his clipboard and stuck his paperwork under his arm. "Okay, let's go. You got a visitor. For your own sake, level with him. He's your last chance, princess."

"A visitor?" Fear lanced a path through Joan. "A him? I don't want to talk to him. I like it in this room. I want to stay here."

Mackleman chuckled as he began unlocking her irons. In his broad East Texas accent, he wisecracked, "Well, we here at the Women's Correctional Resort and Beach Club do try to make our inmates' visits pleasant. So we hope you also enjoy your little chat with the nice deputy sheriff."

Joan ignored his sarcasm, focusing instead on his last word. "Sheriff?"

"Yes, ma'am. An official visitor. A deputy…as in law-man. Tin badge."

Joan made a face reflective of the sickly feeling in her belly. "Are you sure it's not someone just pretending to be a sheriff?"

Mackleman gripped her arm, hauled her to her feet. "Yeah, *that* happens all the time. It's one big joke after another with those crazy impostors." He then moved her aside two paces and said, "He's legit. I know him. He used to be a Houston cop. Until his wife got killed. Now stand right there."

She did, but frowned in curiosity at the man's off-hand revelation. "His wife got killed? How?"

"Drunk driver. About four or five years ago." With that, he bent over to couple Big Betty to a tattooed, ratty-looking biker babe who'd been on Joan's left. When he drew himself up, he warned, "You ladies behave. Don't make me have to come back over here."

The resulting lurid suggestions and catcalls and obscene kissing sounds—not all of them directed at the big, muscled cop towing her along by the arm—had Joan shuffling rapidly within the confines of her ankle manacles. By the time they'd reached the door, she was pulling Houston's finest behind her. "Hold up, O'Leary. My bulldog's better-mannered on a leash than you are. Now, heel and let this nice man here do his job."

Joan forced herself to be still as she waited for a barrel-shaped guard to unlock and open the door. She should've thought this through, she chastised herself. What did she think the police would do when she confessed to a major crime that was the top story in the nation? Take her to tea? She should've known she'd be subjected to imprisonment and all its…finer points.

"Okay, let's go, Ms. 8-7-6-3-4-1-9." Mackleman tugged her forward. Joan breathed a sigh of relief when the barred door closed behind them with a metallic *clunk*. Free at last from Big Betty's leers and innuendos. A shudder rippled through her at the mere thought of—"This way," her guard directed, cutting off her thoughts and indicating the long hallway ahead.

Joan peered down its deserted length. Tunnel-like, the gray corridor ran on for an uncomfortable last-mile stretch of space. Literally. Hauling in a breath for courage, she minced along in her ankle irons, trying to talk at the same time. "Where're you taking me?"

"To the Harvest Moon Ball. Where else?"

Joan had time only to make a face at the man's answer before he stopped her in front of another metal door, this one labeled Interview Room 3. "Here we are," the guard announced cheerily as he opened the door and handed her inside. "Sit down and behave, O'Leary."

Two paces past the dour cubicle's threshold, Joan clanked to a stop. Her anxious gaze sought every corner. Empty, except for her and Sergeant—a heavy bang jerked her around. She stared at the closed door. Okay, empty except for her. She turned back around, eyeing the gray metal table and two chairs...just sitting there...waiting. Hanging low over these prison-movie props was a bright bulb encased in a dingy conical shade.

Interview room, my foot. Interrogation room. She'd been expecting this. Any minute now, big angry men would come in and yell, and beat her until she confessed. Wait. She'd confessed already. All that was left was to give her a fair trial and then kill her, right?

Don't scare yourself to death before the state of New Mexico gets its chance. Just then footsteps in the hallway stopped in front of the door behind her. Joan tensed, listening. Male voices, male laughter. She strained to hear but couldn't make out their words. She did recognize Sergeant Mackleman's twang, though. Was the other one, then, that tin badge—the sheriff?

Oops. She'd been told to sit down. Stumbling forward à la Frankenstein's monster—or maybe his bride—Joan hobbled to the table's far side and plopped onto the chair that faced the door. Then, watching that closed barrier as if she expected it to bark, she mentally fussed at the madness that had put her here.

Who knew that Mr. LoBianco was a criminal?

There ought to be a job-hunting law that stated, "At the *beginning* of a job interview, prospective employers must disclose to the interviewee the really bottom-line important stuff about themselves." After all, how hard was it to extend your hand in greeting and say, *"Hello, I'm a mob boss*

*and doing all sorts of illegal things that can get us both
killed—or cause me to kill you one day soon. And you
are…?''*

But no-o-o. She'd had to discover that little tidbit for
herself. In a most spectacular and bloody way, too. Hello?
She was a freelance accountant. She did bookkeeping. How
dangerous was that? Well…*real* dangerous—if your boss's
nightclub is a front for organized crime. And it's being used
as a laundry—for dirty money. *Which* she promptly figured
out the first time she did the books. You'd think, with the
billions those guys handled, they'd be more skilled at cre-
ative financing to cover their tracks.

Boy, it didn't get any better than this. All those years
working in the Lane Tag Agency here in Houston to put
herself through college? Wasted. And her degree in ac-
counting? Down the tubes. Just like the stable, independent
life she'd built for herself, the one she'd never had growing
up.

But all those foster homes in Texas now felt a lot less
Oliver Twist-ish than today's accommodations. Joan instantly chided herself. That wasn't fair. Nothing bad had
ever happened to her while in foster care. It was just the
constant moving, the sense of never belonging, the never
feeling loved that had taught her some real-life lessons.
Like self-reliance. And keeping her feelings to herself. And
trusting her heart only to her own keeping. Well, she had
Jack to thank for enforcing that last lesson.

If she could find him, she'd kill him. *Note to self: Refrain
from saying things like "kill him" when the nice sheriff
comes in.* Okay, if she could find Jack the Heart-ripper Ex-
boyfriend Weasel/Ski Instructor, she'd really…yell at him,
boy. He'd begged her, in repeated phone calls, to move to
Taos to be with him. It's great here. You'll love it. All

kinds of work. And nowhere near the traffic and crime that Houston has. Please join me, honey. I love you.

Joan could still hear her last and favorite foster parents, Bob and Pam, pleading with her. Don't go, Joan. You're part of our family. Your life, your friends, your clients—they're all here. And what's Jack? A good-looking heartbreaker. You've known him for three months. He's a waiter—not a ski instructor. Before waiting tables, he was a substitute gym teacher. So what sudden epiphany had him running for the closest ski valley? How stable is that?

But in the end, their pleas had fallen on her love-deafened ears. Jack wasn't the first man to say those words to her, but the results were always the same. Now Joan slumped in her chair, denouncing herself as a hopeless romantic. How hopeless? She'd bought a Mrs. Tea because Mr. Coffee looked lonely just sitting there all by himself on her counter. So she'd packed up and headed for Taos, looking to surprise Jack. Looking for romantic happiness.

And when she got there on that hot August day a month ago—with all her belongings crammed into her old Volkswagen—Jack had indeed been surprised. So had the girl living with him. The jerk. The jerkette. In less than one strained week, those two had cut for Colorado. Joan sincerely hoped they'd fallen off a mountain. So, there she'd been—stranded in Taos. But finally and forever wiser. Her eyes open. And too mortified to face Pam and Bob and listen to their well-meaning we-told-you-so lecture.

So, she'd started over in New Mexico. Less crime, Jack had said. You want crime? Try Mr. LoBianco. Okay, getting mixed up with him hadn't been Jack's fault. Mr. LoBianco had been a paycheck, a job. Well, it had started out that way. But soon, the question of family had come up. She'd spoken of foster homes. He'd seemed…well, happy about that. Now she knew why. He'd probably been thinking that if things went wrong and he had to kill her, who'd know? Or care?

Only *he* hadn't killed *her*. Wasn't irony great? Joan grimaced. This was not going to look good on her résumé which, with its Death Row postmark, would already have one strike against it. Last Job: *Freelance accountant to the mob.* Duration: *One week.* Reason for Leaving: *Killed boss.* Even worse, what had she been thinking, after the bloodshed, to run screaming back to Houston? Okay, she'd panicked, headed for "home." Well, comfortable familiarity, if nothing else. But fleeing here certainly proved to be the ultimate headline for *Duh!* magazine.

Because where's the first place little woodland creatures head when they're being hunted? Their burrow. And who knows that? The big nasty carnivores chasing them—a.k.a., a very upset hit man. Close calls with him just inside Houston's city limits had certainly shown her the error of her ways. Lucky for Pam and Bob and their kids, though, she hadn't reached them before the bad guy reached out to her. With his car and his gun.

Her poor "parents," to have such a stupid "kid" as her. She'd actually called them from a pay phone, but got their answering machine. And hung up without leaving a message when that big black car, just like in the movies, came screeching around the corner. Thinking back on it now, Joan asked herself what she'd been going to say to Pam and Bob. *Hi! You were right—New Mexico was a disaster. But I'm back! By the way, I have a mob hit man trying to kill me. So, can you put me up for a few days? I'll help you barricade your house.*

Unbelievable. She would have led that sociopathic goon right to them. Maybe gotten them all killed. Just as she would've been, had she not jerked around the corner of that convenience store before the bad guy had seen her. And then, when she'd peeked out to see if the coast was clear, she'd instead caught sight of...herself. *Could they find no other picture but the goofy one on her driver's license?* Because it had been plastered all over the front page of some newspapers stacked on a wooden stand.

The headlines had read that she was wanted for questioning in the LoBianco murder case. Yes! And *that* was, when? Four days ago, she'd turned herself in to the police and confessed. And those fun guys! Two detectives—Hale and Carter. Clearly amused with her story, the fatherly types had counseled her. Look, miss, maybe you got head problems, maybe need some medication, some kinda help? You don't wanna do this. Let us call a sheriff friend out in Taos and tell him your story, see if we can cut you loose.

Joan recalled her desperation over that revolting development. So, to ensure her arrest, she'd lunged for an officer's gun. And thereby won her all-expenses-paid trip to the safety of a jail cell.

A key scraped into the metal door's lock. Joan snapped back to the present, sat up straighter. The door began inching open, the conversation in the hallway became louder. Apparently, whoever this was, he was still talking to someone outside as he entered. So he was a sheriff, huh? Would he be like the bad one of Nottingham? she wondered. Or one of the good ones, like from the Wild West cowboy movies?

As if it mattered. Because, more to the point, whoever this sheriff was, he held her life in his hands.

STILL FACING THE PRISON hallway and gripping the doorknob of Interview Room 3, Dan spied the ambling approach of Detectives Hale and Carter. He felt the years fall away as he called out to the middle-aged men. "There you are—the men of the hour. It's about time. I was just about to go in.''

"So go in," Jack Carter called out, gesturing with his thick bearlike hands. "Just because you haven't seen us in five years doesn't mean we've got to hug and cry. One phone call to you doesn't make you family, you know.''

Dan chuckled. "I sure as hell hope not." Then he roughly embraced the two older men—the light and the bane of his long-ago rookie existence in Houston. "How the heck are you two guys?''

Ed Hale pulled back with his partner and darted self-conscious looks up and down the hallway, as if making certain no one had seen their male bonding. "I'm good. Carter here had some heart trouble, though.''

Concern edging his eyes, Dan focused on Jack. "You okay?''

"Yeah," Jack replied, shaking his head. "That's his new joke. He means I don't have a heart, that they couldn't find one. I haven't had any problems. How about you, kid? You doing okay?''

The sudden tightening in Dan's throat caught him off guard. Jack alluded, he knew, to Marilyn's death five years ago. "Yeah. You know me." Then he deflected the emotion with, "So, what's the real reason you guys sucked me into this extradition?''

Ed shrugged his sloping shoulders and scratched his graying crewcut. "Nobody sucked. We just called your boss and asked. You always this cheerful with your old friends?''

"Only those who want me to sacrifice my career.''

"Aw, come on, kid, it's not that bad." Hale looked Dan up and down. "You've aged. So, you still a crusader for justice?''

Just as he'd suspected. Dan stepped back out into the

hallway. The use of that old nickname, given him by them, could not be good news. Closing the solid door behind him, he said angrily, ''All right, what gives here?'' A file folder in one hand, he crossed his arms over his chest and glared from Hale to Carter. ''Is my being here an elaborate scheme to collect on that old bet?''

The veteran detectives exchanged a look fraught with innocence, but then Carter gave them away. ''You always said if we found an innocent suspect, we should call you and you'd buy us steak dinners. We did, and we did. And now you are.''

''Found one. Called you. And you're buying,'' Hale clarified.

Dan looked from one detective to the other, and tried his best not to grin back at them. They hadn't changed a bit. Just gained a few more years, lines, and pounds. ''I'm buying? Go to hell.''

''Jack's Bar and Grill will do. A bet's a bet, kid. Miss O'Leary has motive and opportunity. A prosecutor's dream. Only she's innocent,'' Carter assured him, cuffing Dan's shoulder. ''Make mine a Texas T-bone. Seventy-two ounces.''

''Seventy-two ounces?'' Dan repeated, suddenly feeling like a lone wrestler caught in a tag-team tourney. ''And how can you be so sure—of her innocence, I mean?''

''We know, don't we, Carter?'' Hale turned to his partner, but jerked a thumb in Dan's direction. ''The kid here said crime was cut-and-dried, black-and-white. No gray areas. If there's enough evidence to arrest a guy, he's guilty. No such thing as a smoking gun in an innocent person's hand. Or circumstantial evidence. The boy was cocky, had all the answers. Remember how he was?''

Leaving Dan out of the discussion, Carter answered his partner. ''I sure do. We've been holding on to that bet all

these years, too. And now...we got him.'' Finally, he
turned to the topic of their exchange and asked, ''You still
that young idealist, Dan? If it looks like a duck, walks like
a duck—''

''And quacks like a duck, then it's a duck,'' Dan finished
for him. ''I just love hearing my words come out of your
mouth, Carter. Let's just say I was older and wiser back
then, more sure of the world. Now I'm not so sure of anything.''

''Shoulda said so on the phone,'' Hale retorted.
''Could've saved yourself the trip. And the money. 'Cause
we've got an innocent kid right behind that door who's
been charged with Murder One. She's going to earn us
those steaks. And I got—'' he fished around in a pocket of
his wrinkled slacks and finally produced a wadded-up bill,
which he unrolled and eyed ''—five dollars that says you'll
be convinced of her innocence in less than thirty minutes
and killing yourself to get her off. From the charges, I
mean.''

''Wait,'' Dan ordered, holding up a hand before they
could solidify this new bet. ''I'm not here to question
her—just take her back.''

Carter grinned. The man never grinned. Now Dan was
scared. ''Oh, you'll want to take the time to question her,
all right,'' he assured Dan, nodding all the while. ''Wait
until you see her.''

Dan's eyebrows rose. ''Yeah? Good-looking?''

''A knockout,'' the detectives bleated together.

Dan eyed them, turned to eye the door behind him, and
then focused again on the old guys who'd been the first to
teach him how to stay alive in the police business. They
were also the ones who'd spoken personally with Sheriff
Halverson and convinced his boss that only he could pick
up this prisoner. ''You're on,'' he told them. ''Wait here.''

The two exchanged a grin laden with amusement. Shaking his head, Dan again opened the door to Interview Room 3 and stepped in. His gaze went immediately to his prisoner. *Bam!* The bare-knuckled fist of first impression conked him right between the eyes. Words and thoughts failed him. As did breathing. When he was able, he exhaled. Hale and Carter weren't kidding. She was a knockout.

You're staring, Hendricks. Say something. Dan nodded his head in introduction. "Morning, ma'am. I'm Dan Hendricks, deputy sheriff of Taos County. I'm here regarding your extradition to New Mexico to face the murder charges pending against you in the death of Tony LoBianco."

Her only reaction was a widening of her eyes. Aware of the listening detectives behind him, Dan tried again. "Do you understand what that means...extradition? The crime was committed in New Mexico, so that's where the case will be tried. Remember the papers you signed, stating you agreed to allow Texas to release you to go back? That's extradition. And why I'm here. The taking-you-back part."

The scared-looking, angel-faced innocent on the other side of the desk nodded. "I understand."

"Good. And I understand you've waived your right to have an attorney present during questioning—now or at any other time?"

She puckered her mouth and averted her gaze to a wall, showing him a long, thick auburn ponytail. "Yes. I don't need one. I did it."

Startled to hear a suspect in a capital crime blurt her guilt, Dan jerked around and saw Hale's and Carter's smirking expressions. He told them, "Go get a cup of coffee. I'll find you later," then closed the door in their faces and turned back to his prisoner. "Ma'am, 'I did it' is the dictionary definition of when you need an attorney. So, are you going to plead guilty and forgo a trial?"

She shrugged. "I haven't thought that far ahead. Hopefully, it won't come to that."

Dan's frown deepened. "It *will* come to that—and soon. The Houston P.D.'s dropped the charge against you for grabbing that officer's gun. And you've signed the extradition papers. So now we're out of here."

"Then let's go," she said, sounding as if she'd just agreed to a date.

Completely insane. "You do understand that New Mexico has the death penalty? Lethal injection?"

Again she nodded. "Yes, I do. But it won't come to that. I have faith in the legal system."

Dan raised an eyebrow. "Which is why you're refusing legal representation, right? So, tell me, why *are* you doing this?"

Puzzlement lined her otherwise smooth forehead. "Doing what?"

Suddenly peeved with his old buddies for putting him in this position, much less this city, Dan ran a hand over his mouth and took a deep breath. "Look," he began as he approached the table and pulled out the chair facing her. He sat down, flopped her case file onto the table between them, saw her gaze flit to it and then back to his face. "Did you see those two detectives out in the hallway just now?"

She chuckled without humor. "Oh, yes. They laughed, tried to talk me out of my confession."

Dan nodded. "I heard. They're friends of mine. We worked together when I was on the force here five years ago. And now they're asking me to stick my neck out for you. To put it on a legal chopping block, so to speak."

"Why would they do that? That's not very nice."

"Agreed." Getting down to business, Dan shed his navy blue windbreaker and tossed it on the tabletop. He saw her mark his shoulder holster and then meet his gaze again. "So what are we going to do about it, Miss O'Leary?"

2

DAN'S PRISONER SHRUGGED, gesturing narrowly with her handcuffed hands. "'We,' sheriff? It's your call, not mine. But what are they asking you to do—bust me out of here?"

Just picturing that great escape made him chuckle. "They would, if they thought you'd go. But they're convinced you wouldn't take off, even if we opened all the doors and turned our backs." He waited. Her chin came up a notch; she had trouble meeting his gaze. Just as he'd been told to expect. So, he pressed his point. "Is that true?"

She shrugged and said, "It might be." But then challenged him. "Look, your friends are nice family men. They told me about their daughters, about how they think I'm a nice kid. They just don't want to believe I'd...do what I did. I think that's sweet of them. But—and I'm sure you've realized this, too—they're asking you to jeopardize *your* badge. Not theirs."

"Amen." Dan leaned back in his chair, just enough to lift its front two legs off the floor. He crossed his arms over his chest. "And there's not a whole lot I'm willing to risk it for."

"No one in *this* room is asking you to."

Dan narrowed his eyes, considering the red-haired enigma in front of him. And decided to try something else. "Look, I personally don't care if you're innocent or guilty. It's not my job to prove or disprove it. All I care about is *A*—you say you did it. And *B*—we need a viable suspect.

So *C*—we're happy to do business with you. But I do have one concern, Miss O'Leary.''

''And that is?''

''And that is the taxpayer money and man-hours I've spent processing you out of here. See, I don't like Houston. I didn't ever think I'd be back. And yet, here I am—on your account. I've had to relearn Harris County's courthouse floor plan to get you all signed and stamped. Definitely not a day at the beach. So don't get to Taos and change your mind. I would not be a happy camper. Neither would Sheriff Halverson, my boss.''

She frowned, as if peeved. ''Don't worry. I won't change my story and make you look bad. We can't have that.''

Dan dropped his chair to all fours and leaned over the table, his arms resting atop it. ''So I can trust you to continue to put *your* neck in a noose for *me* and that legal system you trust? I appreciate that, Miss O'Leary. Anything to avoid looking incompetent to the public.''

Her frown deepened until her bottom lip had no choice but to poke out stubbornly. ''Is this the reverse-psychology part of the interview where you get me to change my story?''

Dan shook his head, jumping in with both barrels. ''You're not listening. I *don't* want you to change your story. I'm making sure you understand you're *not* to withdraw your confession, you're not to make me and my department look like fools. Especially with the sheriff's re-election campaign in full swing right now and looking a little shaky because of this case.''

His prisoner's delicate jaw set stubbornly. ''Oh, I see—politics.'' Her mouth worked, but then she said, ''You don't mean any of that. Or you wouldn't even have brought up your friends' doubts. Am I right?''

Dan allowed his expression to give nothing away.

"Could be. Let's say I do stick my neck out for you, it wouldn't be as far as you've already stuck yours out. I'd probably lose my badge, my job. But you could lose your life. Can you tell me why you're so willing to do that?"

That got her. Her expression slipped, casting fear at the edges of her mouth, around her eyes. She tried to raise her hands, but her cuffs prevented it. "It wasn't like I had a choice, sheriff."

"Deputy," he corrected. "And why didn't you?"

"Because—" She inhaled deeply, looked very troubled, tried again. "Because…I did it," she said quickly on her exhaled breath.

Dan slouched back, drumming his fingers on the tabletop as he stared at her, wondering if she was protecting someone. If so, she was either extremely noble or incredibly stupid. And he'd already been in this room long enough to know she wasn't stupid. Far from it. Then she was noble. How admirable. But what about himself? What was he thinking, sitting here trying to get her to change her story, to say she was innocent? *Are you so concerned because she's a looker? Or because she looks scared to death? And helpless? And innocent?*

Great. A woman in jeopardy who needed his help. Dan didn't require a department shrink to point out to him why he was reacting to that situation. He hadn't been able to save his wife's life five years ago, so he'd save this woman's. Did Hale and Carter drag him here, force him into this situation, just to make him feel something again? To care?

Huffing out his breath, running his fingers through the military cut of his hair, Dan eyed her green-eyed stare and childlike pout. And got mad. "Are you a moron or some kind of a nut, Miss O'Leary?"

Her mouth dropped open, an involuntary noise escaped her. "What?"

Dan shrugged. "It's a legitimate question in light of what's happened in Taos in the week since the murder. My little corner of the world is now the stomping grounds for the national press corps. And they're laughing over our efforts to get a murder-one rap to stick to a suspect. Why? Because of six nutcase 'confessions' previous to yours. Every one of them was a loony looking for media attention or publicity for some cause."

Her eyes sparked with rising temper. "Not to worry. I'm none of the above, Sheriff." Then, suddenly blinking, she puffed her breath out and upward, trying to blow a wisp of bangs out of her eyes.

He watched her struggle and commented, "All right. Then you're either guilty or innocent. Let's say you're innocent, but you saw something. And the bad guys forced you to say you killed Tony, or be killed. Am I getting warm?"

She shook her head no, even as tears came to her eyes. Not so much from emotion, he reckoned, as from that hair still poking at her eyes. Irritated to the extreme with her story and her distracting gestures, Dan reached across the table and swiped the offending wisps away. She tensed at his touch. His fingers froze against the warm, taut skin covering her forehead. He looked deep into her eyes, saw a world of hurt and fear there. He'd seen that look before. And knew he couldn't walk away. Damn that Hale and Carter.

Against his better judgment, against his years of police training and experience, Dan heard himself losing not only his bet with the two detectives, but also his professional detachment and, quite possibly in the near future, his life. "Look, I don't know why you're doing this, why you're

so determined to throw your life away. But whatever your
reasons—and I don't care what they are—they're not good
enough. Not for me. So, like it or not, I'm going out on
that legal limb with you.''

Joan O'Leary eyed him, crinkling the skin at the corners
of her eyes. Then she inched back from his touch. Grateful
for that, Dan sat back, too. Then she spoke. Her voice was
flat, emotionless. ''I can't let you do that.''

''Can't let me what…touch you? Fair enough. But help
you? You can't stop me.'' With that, Dan reached for her
file and opened it, began sorting papers, looking for the
report on her initial interview. He also awaited her chal-
lenge. It didn't come. A secret grin tugged at his mouth.
Gotcha.

As he scanned the pages, he warned himself to remember
that his job consisted solely of placing her in his custody
and taking her back to Taos. *And turning her over to the
questionable mercy of the sharp-toothed, very fallible legal
system she said she trusted.*

With that thought, tension suddenly banded Dan's forehead and squeezed tight. He put his fingers to his temples
and rubbed as he concentrated on finding the page he
needed. Aha. There it was. Buried in the back. Should have
known. He held it up, skimmed it. ''Lovely. Carter's
chicken-scratch handwriting.'' He glanced at his prisoner,
saw her quizzical expression. ''Yes, I talk to myself. I also
answer.''

With that, he ignored her again, instead turning his attention to the report in his hand. He searched for one over-
looked detail that screamed discrepancy, maybe even innocent. One beyond-a-reasonable-doubt detail that he could
use. Because everyone from the voters to the governor,
from the Taos Chamber of Commerce to the national press,
howled for an arrest.

And Sheriff "Big Ben" Halverson, caught right in the middle of the outcry, was not going to sit patiently through half-baked theories of innocence on Nutty Confession Number Seven. One more headline about his department arresting a suspect, only to have to turn him—her—loose, and the longtime sheriff was dog meat.

And Ben didn't deserve that. Yeah, he was gruff and rough, like an old grizzly bear. But he had a teddy bear's heart. A virtual one-man institution in New Mexico and one hell of a respected sheriff. *Until,* that is, Tony LoBianco got himself killed in Big Ben's jurisdiction. When a big-time mobster, who was about to become a big-time informant, gets murdered, someone's got to take the flak.

And look at you, Dan chastised himself, *hunting for a way to make the sheriff look sillier. The very man who called you with a job after Marilyn's death, who gave you a chance to leave Houston with dignity, to go home and take care of Grandpa. Ben—who stepped in when your father was never around, when you were a cocky teenager and always in trouble. The man who believed in you when no one else did. He maybe saved your life, the way you were headed back then. And now look at what you're doing.*

Feeling lower than dirt, Dan slumped, let the report flutter out of his hand. What *was* he doing? He owed Ben Halverson. Not Joan O'Leary. He gazed across the table at her. Looking very young, very soft and very innocent, she watched him intently. Another unbidden surge of protectiveness surprised him. Those story-starved reporters in Taos would take her apart. And then they'd dismantle the entire sheriff's department—from Ben on down.

How *would* she hold up against a mob of reporters, all shouting questions at her? Maybe he ought to test her mettle. Maybe he'd get lucky and she'd blurt out who really killed Tony LoBianco. Because she didn't do it. He closed her file and crossed his arms over his chest. Time to discredit her story. "All right, let's say I believe you, that you are guilty. Why'd you kill him?"

Joan O'Leary blinked. "Why'd I kill him?"

"I asked you first."

She looked everywhere but at him. "Um, I killed him...because he was...cheating on me."

"Cheating on you?" Dan said. "You told Carter and Hale you were his new bookkeeper, that you'd worked for him for a week. Now you two were lovers? For how long?"

She looked him right in the eye and said, "For that same week."

"You work fast, I'll give you that. Okay, so you juggled more than his books. You two had a thing going. For a week. And he was already cheating on you." His unspoken insinuation was on purpose. She couldn't be all that "good" if her lover strayed so soon.

She took the bait. Snapping forward in her chair, she retorted, "I didn't *juggle* books or anything else. Maybe he was cheating on *her* with me. Maybe I didn't know about her until I caught them together. Did you think about that?"

"No, but that's good. So that's why you offed him? One week into a relationship and you loved him that much, enough to kill him?"

Her defiant attitude bled a little. She frowned, as if wondering where to go from there. Then she nodded. "Yes. That's it—a crime of passion."

"Was it?" Well, he was hating that whole idea worse and worse. Scumbags like LoBianco shouldn't get women like Joan O'Leary. Reminding himself that he believed she was lying, that none of this had actually happened—beyond her working for the man—Dan asked, "Who was he with?"

"Who?"

Dan uncrossed his arms and snapped, "Tony Lo-Bianco—your lover. When you caught him cheating, who was he with? We're burning daylight here, Miss O'Leary."

And she snapped right back. "I don't know her name. We were never formally introduced...under the circumstances."

"Okay, I can buy that. So, who do we look for, since we'll need to question her? What'd she look like? And I'm assuming here you didn't kill her, too, and dump her body somewhere?"

"No, I didn't kill her or dump her body. But what'd she look like...let's see. Pretty. Tall. Pretty tall. I don't remember."

Dan almost jumped out of his chair. "You caught your lover with a woman you remember only as pretty tall? Not buying it. Say you were my lover, and I caught you cheating on me. I promise you—given the way I'd feel about a woman who looks like you—that I'd know exactly what that guy looked like. Down to the smallest detail. Right before I took him out."

Silence...of a funereal quality...thickened the air between them. Too late, Dan's brain kicked in, replaying for him everything he'd just said—and revealed. *Oh, hell.* Worse, he found he couldn't look away from Joan O'Leary's assessing green eyes. Even when his face heated up. Good thing she couldn't hear the guilty thumping of his heart.

Finally, his suspect raised a dark brown eyebrow. "All that anger," she began, speaking slowly, deliberately. "All that...passion you just expressed? That's exactly how I felt. And what you said you'd do? I did."

Except for an eyebrow raised in skepticism, Dan ignored her statement. "I'm going the long way around for my next question, so bear with me. I told you I'm a deputy in the

Taos County Sheriff's Department. In that capacity, I patrol the city of Taos. Which means I've driven across every mile and down every street. It's not that big. Okay, here's the question. How come I never saw you—with or without Tony? Him, I saw. I kept an eye on him. But I never saw you.''

She slid her gaze away from his face and shrugged. "I haven't lived there long. But there's no reason why I should come to your notice. You're the law, and I'm pretty law-abiding. Well, except for this." She indicated her hand-cuffed condition. And then quietly added, "Maybe Taos is bigger than you think."

He chuckled, but not so much from humor. "Maybe it is. Did you move there from here? Is Houston home?"

A funny-sad look claimed her features. Dan didn't know what to make of that. But finally, she nodded yes.

"Why'd you leave?"

"Why'd I leave?" she repeated and then chuckled, shaking her head. "Because I'm a hopeless romantic. My boyfriend Jack said—" She stopped and stared at him, blanking the emotion from her face. "I needed a…a change of scenery."

Dan sent her a sidelong look. "So besides Tony, you have this boyfriend Jack? Where's he? How does he figure in all this?"

A bleat of laughter escaped her. "Not at all. He's history." Her grin instantly flipped to a frown as she rushed on. "Not 'history' as in dead. 'History' as in he's in Colorado. I didn't kill him."

"Glad to hear it. So, Jack's history, and you needed a change of scenery." Dan pointedly looked around the room. "I'd say you got it."

Her answering laugh was surprising. And low and husky. "No lie. Check me out." She raised her manacled hands.

Dan let that pass, seeing as how that throaty laugh of hers was skipping over his nerve endings. "Tell me what you saw on the night of the murder."

She arched an eyebrow. "You mean what I *did?*"

He grinned at her quickness. "Okay. What you did."

She studied him a moment and then launched into her tale. "I had some questions about the books. It was my first time to do them, and things didn't add up. So when the club closed that night, I took them to—um, I mean I went to see Mr. Lo—Tony…like I always did. We had a date. But that night, I was…later than usual. And I heard some noises in the back room. When I went there, I saw—" She clamped her lips shut against her next words.

Dan sat very still. "Like I said, what'd you *see?*"

Her face puckered. From a bloody memory? She struggled for a moment but managed to blurt out, "Just read my statement. It's all in there."

Dan tapped a finger on her case file. "I did, but I don't believe it. In fact, I'm ready to recommend we cut you loose right now."

"No!" Joan O'Leary shouted, surging forward, leaning over the metal table. Dan drew back, instinctively reaching for his gun. But stayed that action when he looked into her pleading green eyes. "Please don't turn me loose. You've got to believe me. Please."

Working her panicked state, Dan calmly shook his head, affecting a detachment he didn't feel. "I'm trying, but you don't give me much to work with. Your story falls apart with only a few questions. But even if it was ironclad, I'd still have one huge, glaring problem. And that is, there's no way you repeatedly *stabbed* to death a big, tough guy like Tony LoBianco. No way."

She stared mutely at him for long seconds and then said,

"That's exactly my point—one for the legal system to figure out."

"Figure out what? You place a lot of blind faith in that system, Miss O'Leary. And maybe you shouldn't. Yeah, it works and works well. But it's populated by people, and people make mistakes. They're prone to oversights, to misjudgments that can get you killed. I've had firsthand experience with that."

She seemed to harden some with her shrug. "So have I. I was entrusted at a very early age to our legal system, Sheriff. I know how it works, what it can and cannot do. It's not perfect, but it's all I've got. I'll take my chances."

Dan ran a hand over his mouth, exhaled loudly. "Look, I don't mean to bust your chops with all this. I'm just trying to sort it out. If Tony had been stabbed from behind, you and I would already be on the road. But he wasn't. The wounds are all frontal. In his chest. The medical examiner says the first wounds weren't fatal, that Tony fought back. That's verified at the crime scene. And yet, here you sit, a week later, with not the first bruise or cut or injury of any sort."

She raised an eyebrow. "How do you know? All you can see are my face and arms."

"I was going by the report made of your physical condition when you were processed in."

She stiffened and immediately began turning red. "You *saw* that? You *read* it? There's an actual *report* in my file of that woman examining me? I cannot believe this." Her green eyes begged him to tell her it wasn't true.

He couldn't do that. And she could see it on his face. Uncomfortable in the extreme, Dan quickly moved on. "Back to Tony fighting his assailant. Guessing at your weight, I figure he had way over a hundred pounds on you. So how do you explain that?"

Looking pretty green around the gills, she blurted, "Genetics, I guess. Or maybe he ate more than I did."

"What?" Then thinking back to his question, Dan chuckled. "I wasn't asking why he was bigger than you. I meant how do you expect me to believe that you killed him."

Her gaze was now steady and focused. "I didn't know I had to convince you. You said it earlier—your job is to take me back to Taos. When are you going to do that?"

Insulted by her dismissive words, as much as by her flippant attitude toward her own life, Dan's expression hardened. Here he was, trying to save her life, and she wanted to get on with the road trip? "So don't help yourself. It's no skin off my nose."

Surprisingly, she backed off. "Look, I'm sorry. It's just that I don't know what else to tell you. If you think I'm lying, that I didn't do it, then fine, keep investigating. Keep looking for other suspects. But until you find one, I'm your man—woman. I've confessed, and I won't retract my confession. Because outside these walls, I'm as good as—"

"Dead?" Dan finished for her, suddenly sure he was onto something here. Just as Hale and Carter suspected, too. "Are Tony's buddies after you? Come on, Miss O'Leary, tell me the truth. You need to trust somebody."

"Now *that's* funny." She chuckled as though at a private joke. She looked away, shook her head at the blank wall to her right.

Dan searched her profile, hoping for a clue as to what made her tick. But what he saw, what he felt was…fear for her, that resurgence of protectiveness. And yeah, a whole lot of physical attraction. She was the only good-looking convict he'd ever seen…with all that auburn hair, that fringe of bangs across her forehead. The sweep of those high cheekbones. The perfect nose and full lips.

As if she felt the weight of his stare, she pivoted her head on that swan neck of hers and locked gazes with him. Dan caught his breath. Her green eyes shamed Ireland for richness of color. And shot to hell what might have remained of his professional detachment. Looking her right in the eye, leaning toward her, he crooned, "You don't look like a murderer."

She stiffened and pulled back…defensively, shutting him out. "Murderers have a look?"

"Yeah. They do. A look and a profile. And you don't fit either." With that, Dan scooted his chair back and crossed his legs, an ankle atop his opposite knee. Then, trying to catch her off guard, he said abruptly, "You never had a thing with Tony. There was no other woman. You just worked for him. So maybe you're mob, too. Maybe you played with Tony's numbers, played him for a fool and got him killed. Maybe you have ambitions and found a way to move up some in the organization."

She nearly came out of her chair. "Me—in the mob? I don't think so. And I did *not* get him killed. In fact, until that night I had no idea that Mr. LoBianco—Tony—was a—" She pressed her lips together and glared at him.

Again, Dan finished for her. "A mob boss from Vegas? You had no idea your lover was a what, Miss O'Leary?" Her frowning expression emphasized her high cheekbones and generous mouth. Dan shifted his weight, forced himself to focus on her eyes. "What are you *really* afraid of?"

She again attempted to cross her arms. Grimacing when her chains prevented it, she let her hands fall limp. "I'm not afraid of anything."

"Everyone's afraid of something," he said quietly. "We just need to work on whatever it is that's scaring you." In the face of her defiant silence, Dan stood up, shrugged into his windbreaker. Then he turned away and stalked to the locked door. He pressed a button on the intercom set into the wall and spoke into it. "Griffin, I need your keys, man."

He stepped back when a key turned in the lock. The door opened to reveal a potbellied, balding guard who dangled a ring of keys from his hand. Griffin sorted through them, found the one he wanted and held the ring out by that key. Dan took it, saying, "Thanks. We'll be out of here in a minute."

The guard nodded, cut his gaze to the prisoner then exited the room, closing the door behind him. Dan approached his prisoner, crooking a finger at her and saying, "Stand up, please."

She stood. But did she have to stare up at him with that scared-doe expression on her face? She didn't ask, but Dan reassured, "I'm just taking Houston's cuffs off you. Their property. They stay here."

She tensed, breathing shallowly. "Are you...cutting me loose?"

There it was—that fear in her voice that sliced like a knife through his gut. Dan shook his head. "No. You've been arrested and charged. Only the D.A. out in Taos County can cut you loose." Then, taking a big risk, he did something every rookie cop knew better than to do. He knelt in front of her to unlock her ankle manacles. This exposed his head and neck to danger, should she decide to attack him. But he knew she wouldn't. Just knew, that's all.

Pulling the irons free of her, he chanced a look up at her face. Miss O'Leary's classic features still looked very troubled. Dan raised an eyebrow. "I *can* trust you not to try to escape, can't I?"

She nodded. "As much as you can trust any cold-blooded killer."

Dan fought the grin that tugged at his lips. "Point taken. But to do that, you'd have to jump out of a perfectly good airplane. Would you?"

"Only if it was on the ground. Otherwise, not without a perfectly good parachute."

"A smart aleck. I like that in a prisoner." With that, Dan straightened up to his near-six-foot height. This put the top of her head at his chin. He hoped that point wasn't lost on her. He also hoped she remembered the 9-mm he had strapped in its shoulder holster under his windbreaker. "For the record," he added, "the Cessna *will* be in the air. And you *won't* have a parachute."

Her puzzled frown deepened. "Why not? I mean, why would I need one? And what Cessna?"

"Hold still," was Dan's only answer. He then worked to unlock her handcuffs and the waist-chain. This close to her, he caught her scent—warm and clean. But sweet somehow. Heady stuff. He glanced up…met Joan O'Leary's openly-staring-at-him green eyes. His gaze slipped from her eyes to her mouth. *Get a grip, Hendricks.* He did, taking a giant step back and speaking as nonchalantly as he could. "We'll be flying back to New Mexico now."

"We will?" Looking like a ponytailed little girl questioning an adult, she raised her chin to gaze up at him. "I convinced you that I'm…guilty of murder?"

"I didn't say that, now, did I?" He reached under his jacket and pulled out the handcuffs attached to his belt. When he reached for her, she pulled her wrists to her chest, shook her head. Like a child defending herself against further hurt. A sense of helplessness had Dan firming his lips into a straight line and saying tightly, "Protocol. Hold out your hands."

Grimacing right back at him, she offered up her

wrists—and a fuss. "As if I could do anything to you. You're more than twice my size."

Finally. Safe territory. And precisely the point he wanted to make with her. "So was LoBianco."

Her expression changed to wary. "But you have a gun."

"So did LoBianco."

A grain of fright shadowed her expression. "He did?"

"Yep. I'd think you'd know that." Dan locked the cold irons around her child-size wrists. And hated like hell doing it. Her skin was red and raw. He fought to keep his expression neutral. "All right," he said, "let's go. You and I have some papers to sign. And guess who insisted on holding them? Our favorite detectives. So you'll get to tell Hale and Carter goodbye. And I can pay off an old bet."

3

AS ORDERED by the bossy pilot, Joan had remained quiet for several hours. *Quiet* meaning she hadn't spoken out loud. Her thoughts were another matter. Jeez, what a bare-bones airline. No movie, no magazines, no bathrooms, no beverages. No food. Not even one lousy, hermetically sealed little bag of peanuts. As if she could open one. The only person with enough smarts and muscles to do that—without suffering a stroke while trying—would have to be a cross between a card-carrying Mensa member and a professional wrestler.

So with nothing else to occupy her time or her thoughts, she glanced to her left at Deputy Sheriff Dan Hendricks. This was a whole different side of him she was seeing. Somehow, up here in the wild blue yonder, he didn't seem as intimidating as in the interrogation room in Houston. She could almost forget he was a cop, that she was a handcuffed prisoner in his custody. She found herself wondering what he was like personally. One way to find out. Besides, he'd had things his way long enough.

"You didn't tell me you'd be the pilot," Joan yelled, not sure if he could hear her under those lime-green earphones on his headset. Or over the loud droning of the itsy-bitsy, teeny-weeny little plane's engine.

But apparently the big deputy could hear something because he turned to her, frowning as he moved the earphone to behind his ear and resettled his sunglasses. "What?"

"I said, you didn't tell me you'd be the pilot."

"Ta-da! I'm the pilot."

Joan made a face. "Imagine my relief, seeing as how you keep fiddling with all the controls to this thing."

He surprised her by grinning at her comeback and shaking his head. But he didn't say anything. Just repositioned his earphone and refocused his attention on all those controls.

Well, that went well. She occupied herself with clutching at her coat's too-long sleeves. Thank heavens he'd made her put it on. She thought of another question, which she again yelled out. "Whose plane is this?"

Again he looked over at her. Again he frowned as he moved the earphone away from his ear. "What?"

Joan rolled her eyes. "The plane! Whose is it?"

"Oh. The department's." He reached for that earphone again, but some thought stayed his hand. He looked over at her. "And the answers are—it's a Cessna 421. And we have it because our jurisdiction covers a lot of territory. Yes, most of it's mountainous. Yes, we log more miles in this than we do in our police units. And yes, tax dollars paid for the plane."

Another pause while he stared at her behind the dark amber tint of his aviator sunglasses. "Can I put this back on?" He indicated the earphone.

Well, obviously it irritated him that she was talking to him. So she shook her head and said, "Not yet. Are all the sheriffs in Taos pilots as well as cops?"

"No. Just me. And it's commercial—my pilot's license. I got it before I took this job. There's only one sheriff. The rest of us are deputies."

"Oh. So, a pilot and a cop. A man of many talents, huh?"

Again with the grin—a wide, dimpled, twinkling one that

evoked visions of long nights and twisted bedcovers. "I haven't had any complaints."

Joan swallowed, let his loaded comment slide. "So, do you always provide the shuttle service for prisoners?"

"No. You're special. If your next question is how long until we get there, the answer is we're almost there. Hopefully, we won't be too late."

Before she could stop herself, Joan asked, "For what? You got a hot date?"

He grinned. "Yeah. So do you. With a mob of reporters. Sheriff Halverson's setting up a press conference. You're his grist for the news mill. He's tired of being asked how come we're letting the real murderer get away while we chase down every nutcase making a false confession."

Joan fluffed up like an angry chicken. "I told you, I am *not* a nutcase."

The somber deputy stared at her from behind those glasses. "And?"

"And?" She frowned, thought for a second, came up with it. "Oh. And I didn't make a false confession."

"There it is—the part I don't believe."

"Don't. I don't care." *See if I talk to you anymore.* And she didn't. Not for two seconds, anyway. "Does that mean you'll keep looking into all the evidence and considering other suspects?"

"Tell me why we should, when we have you." His squared jaw, the straight line of his mouth and his sunglass-covered eyes rendered him inscrutable. Then he tilted his head down farther, looking at her lap. Joan followed his gaze, saw her white-knuckled hands clutching her coat. She raised her head, again met his...sunglass lenses. "Would *that* scare you, Miss O'Leary—if we quit looking?"

She relaxed her grip on her jacket and lied, "No." Then added, "What does scare me is being aloft in this gnat of a freezing airplane. Which does not have the first magazine, toilet, bite of food or drink or—'' Suddenly hearing her own whining, Joan got quiet and stared at him a moment. ''Sorry. That's the short list of my present miseries.''

This time his grin was no more than a flash of white teeth. ''I think I know the long one.'' With that, he checked his instrument panel and then turned his attention to the outside world. After one or two quiet, engine-droning moments, he said, ''Hard to believe it's in the eighties down there, huh?''

Well, that was out of the blue. And his first voluntary comment. Joan decided to play along. ''‘Down there?' Oh, you mean on Earth? That *is* Earth I'm looking at, right?''

He spared her a glance. ''Can I add a fear of flying to what scares you?''

Joan made her I'm-not-a-baby face. ''It's not the flying that scares me. It's the crashing part.''

''Yeah, me, too. I was flipping through my student pilot's manual, but couldn't find the chapter on what to do if that happens.'' The teasing twist to his lips made her want to grin right back at him.

But she didn't. She just quipped, ''If you learned the other chapters well enough, you won't need that one.''

He laughed. ''Look at it this way—worrying about crashing takes your mind off your short list, doesn't it?''

''Well, it did. But thanks for reminding me.'' Since he was in the mood for chitchat, Joan felt encouraged to make a voluntary comment of her own. ''You must love being up here. It's beautiful. Does this blue sky go on forever?''

Joan saw his eyebrows wing above his sunglasses. Her stomach lurched. ''Did I say something wrong?''

''No. Not wrong. Just ‘blue skies forever.' My wife used to—never mind. I just didn't expect to hear you say it.''

With that, he slipped his earphone back over his ear, indicating they were through talking.

His wife. Sergeant Mackleman said she'd been killed. A real conversation stopper. So, Joan had two choices—either stare openly at him or look out the window to her right. She decided the window was definitely the lesser of two…evils. So, peering out, looking down, she smiled. Gorgeous. Breathtaking. Earth dressed in early autumn colors. The yellows and reds, the blue rivers, the green fields, the high mountains and—

"Did you really kill your lover, Miss O'Leary?"

"What? I don't have a lover," Joan answered absently, still looking out her side window. Her brain promptly kicked her mental behind. She pivoted to face the lawman to her left. That lime-green earphone was pushed back. His expression said he'd heard her answer. Joan rushed to amend it. "I mean, no. No, wait—not no. I mean, yes. Yes, I killed him. In a fit of passion."

"Oh, that's right. Passion," he drawled, affecting a sober frown as he faced the windshield again.

Joan didn't know what to do. Or say. So, from under the sweep of her lashes, she scrutinized his profile. And wished again he'd take off those sunglasses. She liked his hazel eyes, the way the skin crinkled at the corners when he smiled. And the shape of his face, that stubborn jaw and strong chin. The military cut of his thick, dark hair. His wide mouth—

"Like what you see?"

She froze, held her breath. He hadn't even turned his head, and yet he'd caught her memorizing his features? *A better question to self: Why* are *you memorizing his features?* Her heart knocked around in her chest. The moment stretched as she struggled for something appropriate to say.

But the big deputy beat her to it. "I guess not. My mistake."

"Speaking of looks," Joan said, "why's it so hard to believe I acted in a fit of passion?"

"Well, let's see." He looked over at her, then shook his head and shrugged those broad shoulders. "Nope. Don't see it. Not you. But isn't that the wrong term? Isn't it 'the throes of passion?' Or 'a fit of temper'?"

Forget the semantics. Joan zeroed in on his insult. "You don't think I can be passionate?"

He shrugged, like no big deal. "I said *passionate* wasn't the right word. I meant you don't seem—"

"I know exactly what you meant that I…don't seem." Put out with his assessment of her, Joan scrunched down in her seat and brooded. She'd show him passionate. Turn him every way but loose. Without a second thought, she blurted, "Not that it's any of your business, but I can be as passionate as the next woman—even more so. And don't you forget it."

A husky chuckle preceded his words. "I won't. I'm just glad to know that all that red hair and those green eyes aren't wasted on someone with no fire."

Slightly mollified, more than a little flattered and feeling ridiculous that she would be either of those things, Joan tamped a lid on her temper. She even managed to draw in her poked-out bottom lip. "I have fire."

The deputy's chuckle became a laugh. "I'll take your word for it."

She sat up and looked over at him. "Guess you'll have to."

The lawman nodded. "Guess I will. Where you're going, you'll never have a chance to prove yourself." He then turned a three-billion-watt grin on her.

Oh, sweet heaven. Tingles went all the way to Joan's

toes. He was temptation on the hoof. Why couldn't they have sent some old guy to get her, instead of this beautiful, sexy man? When he finally looked away from her, Joan worked at cooling her tingly parts. Because if she didn't, she'd end up hijacking this plane and dragging him off to bed. She closed her eyes against that naked, sweaty vision.

When she risked looking at the world a moment later, she sucked in a breath at the gray and gathering clouds that billowed in the distance. How long had they been there? So much for blue skies being forever. She looked over at her pilot, found him a study in square-jawed grimness. That earphone was back in place. She redirected her worried gaze to the clouds in front of their tiny aircraft. They were flying right into the storm's fury.

Suddenly afraid, she blanked out her thoughts of the deputy's skill as a lover, in favor of his technical skill as a pilot. She raised her cuffed hands to capture the deputy's attention. He glanced at her, moved the earphone back. Joan called out, "What do you make of this?"

His lips twitched around a grin as he gazed at her. "Looks like trouble to me."

He wasn't talking about the weather. Feeling her face heat up, Joan looked down, focusing on her jeans-covered thighs. At least he'd allowed her to dress in her own clothes before hauling her out of the Harris County facility. When she felt more in control of her fluttering belly, she glanced up at him. Thankfully, this time his gaze was fixed on the weather. Her own weather fears had her calling out, "You *were* kidding about that chapter on crashing, right? I mean, you're not a student, right? You can handle this?"

He slowly turned his head until his deep amber lenses were directed at her eyes. He nodded. "I *was* kidding, and yes, I can handle this. Or anything else that requires handling. Even you."

Joan's eyebrows shot up. "You're violating the prisoner-slash-jailer relationship."

He looked from her…to the storm…back to her. "The slash-what?"

"Slash-jailer. We need more detachment between us, sheriff."

"This is as detached as it gets in a plane this size. I can't move over."

Joan quirked her mouth in irritation. "Not that. The looks, the innuendos."

"The what? Are you sure you're not flattering yourself?"

"No, I'm not. I mean, yes, I'm not…not flattering myself. I mean I'm sure." She started over. "I mean, all that talk about my passion and you not having any complaints. And that grinning, twinkly look of yours."

"Twinkly look? I've never looked twinkly in my whole life."

Joan jutted out her jaw like a bulldog. "Well, you just did and not a minute ago. I'll thank you to remember that you have a certain responsibility toward me. After all, here I am handcuffed and helpless and stuck in this bathtub-toy airplane with you, and we're about a billion feet off the ground."

"Eighteen thousand."

"Whatever. It's not fair of you to take advantage of me like this."

The man's jaw poked out to match hers. "Take advan— Did I miss something? How in the—? We're strapped into these seats like astronauts. I haven't put a hand on you in *any* way that didn't have to do with my official duty as a sworn officer."

"Don't play the 'official duty' card with me. Remember

brushing my hair out of my eyes? Remember that? You liked touching me. Admit it."

His voice rose. "Admit what? You're the one who—"

At that moment, the Cessna bucked and jumped. The storm had found them. Wide-eyed with terror, Joan clutched her parka's sleeves and riveted her gaze to every action her pilot made.

Muttering under his breath, he repositioned his earphone and checked all the gauges and knobs and stuff on the panel in front of him. Without looking at her, he called out, "Hold on. We're in for some stormy weather."

"Is that supposed to be funny?" Joan cried out as the tiny plane's wings wobbled. If he heard her, he didn't answer her. And if he'd answered her, she didn't hear it—not over the panicked pounding of her heart. Was she safe in his hands? Could she have confidence in him, in his abilities? She looked over at his hands. He was white-knuckling the wheel thingie. *Oh, God.*

Then, unbidden and surprisingly, he began explaining their situation to her. "This is an unseasonal storm for September, but not unheard of. Houston Hobby and Taos both mentioned I might encounter it when I filed my flight plans. Looks like the 'might' part is right. It's might-y big."

She had to agree as she split her gaze between the increasingly dark outside world and the deputy's face. She saw him shake his head as he consulted some gauge doohickey. She stared at the same gauge and then turned to him. As if she'd asked, he glanced over at her and said, "Can't do much but try to make it in. The good news is...if we crash, these strong north head winds will have used up the fuel. So there shouldn't be any fire."

Joan's eyes bulged at his words, which only made him grin. "Just trying to yank your chain, so to speak." Then he sobered. "You locked in your seat belt?"

Joan tested her halter and lap restraints and vigorously nodded her head. Her pilot gave her a thumbs-up sign and then returned his attention to his craft. Thumbs up? Despite the winds, the buffeting they were taking and the dipping and wobbling the itsy-bitsy plane was enduring, he thought things were thumbs-up? Then maybe it wasn't as bad as she feared.

Just then, he surprised her by reaching over to squeeze her shoulder. "We're going to be okay, Joan."

He'd called her Joan. They were going to die. Tears sprang to her eyes. He must have noticed them, because he shook his head, saying, "Uh-uh. None of that. It's not allowed. We're going to be okay. You believe me?"

Joan blinked back her tears and tried to undo her frown. But couldn't. She had to settle for biting her bottom lip and nodding.

Dan faced forward again. "Good. Hang on."

Hang on? Joan searched the cockpit. To what exactly? *He* was the most solid thing about this Christmas stocking-stuffer enveloping them. But he was kind of busy right now. So Joan clutched her parka and closed her eyes, mumbling every prayer she knew. The tossing and tumbling, the up and down, the side to side, her abject fear, all combined to bring on nausea. *Oh, good. Let me throw up. That'll certainly add to the ambience.*

Just then, the deputy blurted out a particularly descriptive curse. Joan's eyelids snapped up like sprung venetian blinds. And admitted he had reason to curse—the Cessna kept balking at staying right-side-up, much less level. She squeezed her eyes shut again. Every muscle in her body locked as she hunched down in her seat and retreated within herself.

Then she heard his voice, realized he was talking. She opened her eyes. He wasn't talking to her. He was speaking into the black mike boom attached to his headset. She heard him say something like Albuquerque Approach. She tried to hear everything, but got only disjointed words and phrases that did nothing to ease her terror. "...primary flight instruments...failed..."—something, something— "...declaring an emergency."

Then he ripped the headset off and called out, "Hang on, Joan. We're going down."

And he wasn't kidding, either. The plane sought hard earth with the straight-arrow, nose-first vengeance of a hurled javelin. Like the man said, they were going down. "We're going to die!"

"Not if I can help it." His voice was grim. His gaze darted with singular intensity from the instrument panel to Mother Nature's fury outside and then back down to the gauges. "Come on, dammit," he urged. Then, as if suddenly remembering he had a terrified passenger, he called out, "I'm trying to bring us in level so we can slip across the snow to a stop. Instead of plowing into the ground and digging our way to hell."

Joan nodded quickly but said nothing. Her heart racing like a stuck motor, she stared at the fast-approaching earth. Bald rocky patches poked through the snow-covered mountain terrain below. That's how close the ground was. She could see that, could make out individual stands of pine, could see white meadows. *This is not happening.*

Too terrified to watch her fate rising to meet her, Joan snapped her desperate attention to Dan. His concentration was singular as he worked to control the Cessna. Finally its nose inched up and up until the craft was more or less parallel to the ground. Only then did he call out to her. Joan didn't catch his words. She strained toward him, needing very much to hear the sound of his voice over the tripping hammer that was her heart.

"I said we're ice-covered right now. That's to be expected. See this wheel I'm holding? It's the yoke. Watch. Very slight back-pressure on it…like this. Nice and easy. I'm heading for that clearing right below us. With any luck, it's deep enough to cushion us. We're going in with the wings in a level attitude. That's all I can do. See you on the other side, kid."

Still staring at him, unable to look away from him, no matter how much she wanted to close her eyes, Joan held her breath and clung to his profile. She'd said it earlier today—her life was in his hands—but she hadn't known then how true that would be.

And that was her last thought before they met the starkest sort of reality in the high-mountain snowfield. The Cessna hit. The world kaleidoscoped into the fractured, fragmented images of swirling trees caught in a spin cycle. The plane pushed through the deep snows covering the meadow. Like a spun bottle in a kissing game, the Cessna swirled across the icy snow. And finally headed directly, sickeningly, with fast-forward swiftness, for the thick trunks of some monster pines.

Joan opened her mouth, thought she screamed. But no sound came out.

4

JOAN SLOWLY, achingly rejoined the conscious world. Something was strapped diagonally across her chest and holding her hunched forward in a seat. Where was she? And why was she staring at her tennis shoes with such intensity? Ditto her ponytail. It hung over her shoulder, brushed her knees. But the worst part was, she hurt all over and felt sick. She looked at her hands. She was also handcuffed. Why?

Then it all flashed back to her. Tony LoBianco. Houston. Dan Hendricks. The plane. The storm. The javelin. Ah, yes. They'd crashed. And my, wasn't she calm about it all? I'm in shock. That's it. *I'm in shock. Or I'm dead. No, I prefer shock. Who wouldn't be shocked?*

Hurting everywhere, she pulled herself upright, wondering why she had to fight gravity to do so. Then she realized that the Cessna tilted to the left. But something, someone, was missing. Where was Dan?

"Dan?" No man, no body, no answer. The door on his side gaped open and, frighteningly, didn't appear to be impeded by contact with the ground. *Don't even tell me we're up a tree.* She swallowed and took a deep breath. Had Dan fallen out to his death? Would she too if she tried to get out?

Squinting at the blindingly bright, snowy world outside the damaged aircraft, Joan assessed her situation. Okay, the storm had abated some, the world was white and long shadows blanketed her, the plane and the trees. So maybe hours had passed. She shivered. She was certainly cold enough for it to have been hours.

Pushing that thought aside, she took in her more immediate surroundings. The Cessna's crumpled nose was bumped against a thick tree trunk. So, it wasn't up a tree at all. It was on the ground because…she looked to her left and then to her right…she could see other thick-bark trunks. And through a clearing in those, some big purple mountains. But where was Dan? Scared now, she all but whispered, "Dan?"

Still no answer. "Dan?" she called out louder, maybe a little hysterically. "Dan, where are you? You didn't leave me, did you?" Which was a pretty stupid thing to say, she realized. Because if he had, he wouldn't be here to answer, now, would he?

Panic set in. *He left me alone and handcuffed in this snowdrift. I'll freeze to death or get eaten by a bear. Oh, please let me freeze all the way to death before I get eaten by a bear.* Stop it. He probably went to get help. Now get the heck out of this Cessna before it catches on fire and explodes. *Good idea.*

Then she remembered Dan saying it probably wouldn't catch fire because of the fuel and winds or something. But still, thinking better safe than sorry, she tugged frantically at her seat belt. With her hands cuffed and moving together like synchronized swimmers, she fought and scratched until she got her restraints unclasped. Shrugging out of them, she pushed her shoulder against the door on her right as she two-handedly fumbled with the latch.

No dice. Stuck. Jammed. Wedged. It wouldn't open. *Great.* Close to tears now, she slumped in her seat and thought about giving up. Then a gust of cold wind drew her attention to her left, to the other *open* door.

Making a face at her own idiocy, she hitched and flipped, in beached-seal fashion, until she could pull herself up out of her seat. The plane lurched. Joan froze in position—on her knees and holding on to the seat back. Then she sucked in a very cold breath. *Don't do this, nice airplane. I'm sorry for everything I ever said about you. Just hold together until I get out. Please?*

When the plane stayed in place, Joan inched her wary way over to the pilot's seat. But her knee slipped, and she lost her balance. She tumbled face-first and squawking right out of the Cessna, rolling and finally landing in a deep drift of oh-so-chilling snow. Slowly, she came to her knees, spitting and hissing and rubbing her numb fingers over her face. A noise behind her jerked her around. The Cessna shuddered and slid a notch down its snowy embankment. Toward her.

Wide-eyed, Joan struggled to her feet and cleared the area in a dead run. Stopping only when she felt she was a safe distance away, she turned back to the disabled airplane. It slipped another notch. She jumped, fully intending to respond to her instinct to flee.

But just then, a spot of orange in the snow, and in the plane's eventual path, caught her eye. She froze, more from sudden realization and fear than from the cold. The deputy hadn't gone for help at all. Far from it. Because there he was. Lying on the ground. And he *needed* help. Her help.

Not liking herself one bit for it, she hesitated, told herself she was free now. Everyone, including Mr. LoBianco's cronies, would think she was dead and that maybe wild animals had carried off her body. She could change her hair and her name and live her life. Be free of her past. Pick a future more to her own liking.

Yeah, and eat her heart out for the rest of her miserable life because she'd left a man to die. What if he was just unconscious? Could she just stand here and watch the plane crush him? Or leave him here, to die of exposure? "Great," Joan huffed. Still, she looked at the orange parka half buried in the snow…then up at the Cessna…and around the expanse of open country surrounding her.

This was her last opportunity for freedom. Already hating herself, she turned away from the crash site, took a step and walked right into a low-hanging branch. "Okay, I was kidding," she said aloud, fighting off pine needles. "Can't even take a joke."

Without asking herself who she was talking to, she turned around and trudged back to the deputy, telling herself she may as well stay with him. God knows, in her stable, boring, adventure-challenged existence, she'd couch-potatoed enough action-adventure TV shows to know that you always stayed with your craft.

By the unconscious lawman's side now, she stared at his broad back and splayed arms and legs. With his face turned toward her, his cheek rested on a pile of snow-dusted leafy undergrowth. Well, she'd gotten one wish—his sunglasses were gone. Another good thing was his face. It wasn't a bloody pulp. That was never good.

She knelt beside him in the snow, feeling the cold wetness penetrate her jeans. She looked him over. What should she do? Maybe feel his neck for a pulse? Sure. Why not? Holding her freezing fingers against his neck, she felt around, found nothing. Seconds and hope ticked by. Joan moved her fingers to another spot on his exposed flesh. And then, there it was. A pulse. Strong and steady. "Yes!" She slumped over him, hugging him for being alive.

When she raised up, she marked how stiff her muscles were, and how low over the mountains the pale sun was. She had to get him up somehow. She raked her gaze over the man's still form. Maybe she'd better check him for broken bones before she tried to turn him over. Surprised, she sat back on her legs. *Look at me. All of a sudden I'm Miss Wilderness Survival. Where's all this stuff coming from?*

After all, nothing in her citified, foster-home-living, un-witting-accountant-to-the-mob lifestyle had prepared her for this. Good thing that, between boyfriends, she'd kept company with her TV, huh? *Strike a blow for the boob tube later, all right? For now, worry about broken bones and then find shelter from the cold.*

Fine. She leaned forward again, moving her manacled hands awkwardly over the deputy's body. He was so warm under his parka and so finely muscled. Under any other circumstances, Joan told herself, this would be a very… touching moment. But not like this. Poor guy. He was out cold and helpless. And here she was…feeling him up.

Clearing her throat, as well as her hormonal thoughts, she rolled him over as gingerly as she could, given his bulk and her cuffed condition. She then brushed the snow off his face and shook his shoulder, calling out, "Dan? Can you hear me? Are you all right?"

Nothing. Joan sank back on her haunches and looked skyward. Great. Now what? Die here with him? *What am I supposed to do?* Find someplace warm. *I know that. But where?* Her gaze directed itself to the crumpled Cessna. *No, thanks.* But there might be blankets inside. And there's the radio. Maybe it works. Sounded like a plan.

But first, she had to get Dan out of the plane's path. She mentally measured his length and breadth. The guy may as well be Gulliver and she a Lilliputian. Was he never going to wake up? This just wasn't fair. She needed him. He was going to help her, save her from herself. Somebody needed to. She couldn't do it herself. She frowned. Did that make sense?

About as much as this. Just when she met someone who was kind and gentle, even funny, someone she thought she might be able to trust, look what happens. She's charged with murder and he gets whacked in a plane wreck. What were the odds? She looked again to the Cessna and frowned. No telling when gravity would wrench it down on top of them. She looked down at the prostrate deputy. And jumped. His eyes were open, but not very focused. He grimaced and mumbled, "What happened?"

Joan slumped in relief, blinked back tears. "Well, remember earlier when we were airborne, how you kept saying it was going to be okay?" She shook her head. "It wasn't. Here's how un-okay it is—you can forget that press conference. We'll *be* the news. Our crash, that is."

He stared up at her. Blankly. *Great. All the lights are on, but nobody's home.* He tried to sit up, but Joan restrained him with her hands on his shoulders. "Don't move. Something besides your Cessna could be broken."

She thought he looked a little less dazed and confused as he pulled himself up onto his elbows. But then he said, "My what?"

She huffed out a cloud of warm breath and pointed at the winged expanse of steel teetering just up the slope from them. "Your Cessna. It's broken. Your taxpayers are not going to be amused."

Dan craned his neck in the direction she pointed. Then his eyes flew open wide. "Holy—!" He jackknifed up, grabbed her around the waist and rolled over and over and over with her. Finally he rolled to his feet...obviously nothing was broken...and brought her with him. Grabbing her arm, he took off like a Boston Marathon legend, dragging her along behind him.

Stopping somewhere in the next county…in Joan's estimation…he let go of her and bent over, bracing his hands against his knees. Breathing hard, looking pale, he croaked out, "Why were you sitting there? We could have been killed."

"You think?" Sarcasm came naturally when she had wet, tangled, stick-embedded hair, was chilled from a roll in the snow and breathless from being forced to sprint at an Indy 500 pace. Between gasps for air, she griped, "What do you think I was doing? I was trying to make sure you were okay before I moved you. But then you woke up and…well, you know the rest."

Looking somewhat dazed again, if not dizzy, Dan plopped down in the snow. "We crashed. I can't believe we made it. But…I was out cold, and you stayed with me?" He stared up at her in a purely assessing way. "That was a pretty selfless thing for a cold-blooded murderess like yourself to do."

She shrugged. "We have our moments." Then she got defensive. "I thought you'd left me first. You weren't the only unconscious victim here. When I woke up, I was still buckled in that plane and contemplating my shoes."

"I'm glad you're okay. But what made you think I'd left you?"

You're glad I'm okay? Joan studied him. He was a nice guy. Then she said, "Because the door on your side was open, and you were nowhere to be seen. Didn't I say that yet?" She then surprised herself by clogging up with tears. To her horror, her chin quivered and her voice wavered. "I thought you'd left me here to die."

Dan's expression softened. "I wouldn't do that." Then he came unsteadily to his feet, put a hand to his forehead, swayed slightly, blinked several times, and then surprised her by reaching for her. "Come here."

From sheer human need, Joan stepped into his embrace. With her cuffed hands held between her chest and his, she pressed her cheek against his coat's zipper and didn't mind its cold roughness against her skin. She clung to his quilted nylon jacket. For the longest time, she stood melded to him, reveling in this feeling of being safe. She closed her eyes and sniffed again and again.

"Joan?"

"Uh-huh?"

"Run." With that, he broke their warm cocoon of an embrace, clutched at the back of her parka and again dragged her with him.

Having to trundle along somewhat like Quasimodo, given his backward grip on her, Joan concentrated on staying on her feet. From behind them came the metallic wrenching and moaning and cracking apart of the Cessna as it apparently worked on its descent. Dan finally slowed and then stopped, swinging his arm around her to steady her. "Look," he commanded.

Joan turned in his embrace and looked. What she saw transfixed her. She could feel the deputy sheriff pressed to her back, but her thoughts were with the dying Cessna. "Oh no. It's going to slide right over that cliff and down the mountain. There go the radio and the blankets."

"Yep," Dan agreed, watching it go. But then he shifted his weight, causing her to look up at him. "How'd you know there were blankets?"

Joan thought about it, shrugged her shoulders. "I assumed. Were there?"

Dan nodded. "Yeah. Why didn't you get them out?"

"It was them or you. I voted for you."

"Then I owe you one." Just then, another metallic groan split the air. "Uh-oh, there it goes." Joan directed her gaze to the last swan dive of the wreckage. Behind her, Dan said, "It'll just be pieces by the time it gets to the bottom. But any search party will be able to see that it slid down this mountain. They'll come up here to find the point of impact."

Joan turned against the pressure of his hold on her and looked up at his rugged jawline. "Just like on TV. So they'll find us, right?"

Still watching the plane crumble and fall, Dan shook his head. "No. We won't be here. If we stay out in the open like this, we'll be plenty dead and frozen by then."

"Or get eaten by a bear." She again twisted in his embrace to take in their snowy, boulder-strewn surroundings. "Do you know where we are? I mean, exactly."

Dan stepped back, tugging her away from him, but still he held on to her arm. "No, but I have a general idea." He then looked skyward. Joan did the same. "Not good. It's starting to snow again. And it'll be dark in a couple hours."

"Lovely." She meant the situation, not the big, fat, lazy flakes salting them and the already white-covered ground.

Dan looked down at her, then at his hand gripping her arm, and finally settled on her cuffed hands. "Why didn't you say something?" With that, he reached up under his parka and produced a set of keys. "Hold your hands up."

Automatically offering her wrists, she kept her gaze firmly on his cold-reddened hands as he released her from her cuffs. He then hiked up his parka and replaced them on his belt.

"Throw those away, because I'm not wearing them again," she swore as she rubbed her bruised flesh. When he let that pass, she knew something was up. She raised her head, caught his unhappy expression as he stared at her red, chafed wrists. She self-consciously dropped her hands to her sides, allowing the parka's too-long sleeves to cover her fingertips. "What now?"

Her words seemed to rouse him. He met her gaze. "Shelter. Warmth." With that, he turned away, his gaze lingering a moment on the valley below them. Then he looked to the mountains and pointed. "See that ridge on the left there, not too far away?"

Joan squinted and frowned in the direction he pointed. "Let's assume I know a ridge when I see one. Which one and what about it?"

"Right there. In that clearing—like a bald spot about halfway up the mountainside? If I'm right about where we are, there's a cabin over there. It's a seasonal place, mostly used in the winter. Probably no one's there, but at least it should have some canned goods and firewood."

She looked and looked, but for the life of her couldn't make out anything. Except the long, blue shadows slowly settling over the white, forested mountainside. She quit trying to find the cabin and looked up at him. "And if you're wrong?"

Hazel eyes serious, he scratched his jaw. "If I'm wrong, we should die quickly." With that, he trudged off to his left, not looking back to see if she followed. "Freezing to death isn't all that bad. You just give up, sit down and go to sleep. And that's the end of it."

Twisting her lips into a grimace, Joan started out after him. "And how would you know that?"

Over his shoulder he called out, "Walk in my boot prints. It'll make your going easier. And I *don't* know, obviously. I'm just going by what the medical examiner says."

Huffing and puffing from the cold that nipped her lungs, and stretching her stride to match his as she hopped from one imprint to another, Joan kept up her end of the conversation. "Medical examiner. Now *there's* a cheery thought."

"Yeah. Old Harry. You'll like him."

Joan stopped in her...his...tracks as she stared at the man's parka-covered back. "I don't intend to meet him, Sheriff."

Her Abominable Snowman guide chuckled. "Deputy. And you will meet him, too. I want him to have you stab a dummy with a knife similar to the supposed murder weapon so he can see if your efforts match those on your lover's body—which we still have in cold storage. Then we'll know if you're lying or telling the truth."

"Fine. As long as I get to pick the dummy, Sheriff."

He stopped and pivoted around to glare at her.

Joan frowned, recalled her words. "Oh. There's a comma between dummy and sheriff."

"It's deputy. And there better be. Now try to keep up." With that, he once again turned his back on her and trudged onward.

With a shrug of her shoulders, Joan followed him, feeling like a snow bunny hopping from one of his boot indentations to the next. She wondered why he had no qualms about her—a cold-blooded murderess—being behind him. She could pick up a rock or a branch or something and whack him over the head.

As if he'd just thought the same thing, Dan stopped and pivoted to face her. Joan pulled up short...about two long strides behind him...and cocked her head. "What?"

"Don't even think it."

Despite her surprise at his words—could he read her mind?—she grinned. "Yes, sir." To herself she added, *He's afraid of me.*

DAN COULDN'T FEEL his toes or the ends of his fingers. His nose was running. His vision was blurred and teary, thanks to the Popsicle-cold wind. Each step was an exercise in frozen agony. His stomach was growling at his ice-chest lungs, threatening to eat them. And the sun was going down.

Better yet, trailing him was a hopping, whining, red-haired self-professed murderess who'd saved his life. Well, at least she'd said that's what she was doing when he'd come to. She could have been hunting for a rock to crush his skull with, for all he knew.

"I'm freezing, and I'm hungry. Where's that cabin you said you saw? Are you sure it wasn't a mirage?" she asked for the eighty-seventh time. "I think right now I could kill a bear with a stick, eat it whole and wear its fur."

Shaking his head, pretending she didn't make him want to laugh, Dan called back over his shoulder, "Just keep up. The cabin should be around this next bend."

"You said that an hour ago. I think the cabin was a mirage, and you're lost, and we're going to die."

That did it. Dan whipped around, saw her startled response, and felt some of the same, seeing how close she was behind him. "For the last time—keep your distance. I have a *gun*. I am *not* lost. We are *not going to die*—at least, *I'm* not. There *is* a cabin close by. And *mirages* occur in heat, like you'd find in a desert. Does it look like we're in a desert?"

Her cheeks and nose as red as her hair, her eyes as green as the pines around them, she shook her head and sniffed, rubbing her sleeve under her nose. "No. Are you afraid of me?"

"Afraid of you?" Aching, tired of her nonstop yapping, and over any desire—to save her or to savor her—that he might have felt earlier, Dan put his hands to his parka-thickened waist. "Why would I be afraid of you? No more questions. Just shut up and be quiet.'' She opened her mouth. Dan jerked his hand up, all but barking, "I know, shut up and be quiet are the same things. Humor me.''

She started to say something again as she pointed to his left. Again he jerked his hand up. "I said, humor me.''

She huffed out a breath that coalesced and hung in the air between them. "Will you just turn around and look behind you, please?''

Dan shook his head. "Not if my life depended on it.''

"Actually, it sort of does.'' Again, she cut her gaze to his left and then flicked it back to his face. "It's the cabin. I think I see it.''

Dan narrowed his eyes, looking her up and down. An unarmed woman less than half his size. And wearing a parka big enough for a Dallas Cowboys lineman. How dangerous could she be? Yeah, well, he'd seen Tony Lo-Bianco's body. And he didn't have any real proof yet she hadn't killed him. "Come here.''

She did, but trudging and sighing all the way. Stopping right in front of him, she looked up into his face. The ice around Dan's heart melted. Poor kid. Her lips were blue with cold. Her jeans were soaked from the knees down and, unlike his boots which kept his feet relatively dry, she had on tennis shoes. Her feet had to be frozen lumps. And she was shivering.

Steeling his sympathetic nature, Dan clutched her by her parka's shoulder seam and pulled her along as he turned around. "Where's this cabin you think you see?'' he asked her, looking this way and that through the massive column-like tree trunks that stood impassive to them and impervious to the cold.

"If you'll let go of me, Sheriff, I'll show you.'' Her words shook with her shivering voice. She hugged herself and hopped in place from one foot to the other. "Like I'm going to run off. Where exactly would I go? If I did run, and as you keep reminding me, you have a gun.''

Dan narrowed his eyes at her...and let go of her. ''All right. Lead on.''

And she did, weaving them unerringly through the dense copse and straight to a small clearing that sheltered...the cabin. Impressed that she'd found it, but prepared to die before he'd admit it, Dan ignored her when she turned to him and swept her arms out to one side, indicating the little house in the fashion of a game-show model.

Grumping under his breath, he brushed by her, intent on finding something he could use to break that padlock on the door. If they weren't inside soon, out of these clothes and in front of a warm fire, they'd be poster children for frostbite. Not giving his prisoner a second thought, Dan searched the cabin's perimeter, kicking aside snow, throwing off tarps. Working his way around to the right, he found firewood stacked against the cabin. Out back, a washtub.

Frustrated, he rounded the far corner. And met up with Joan. Walking toward him, she brandished a crowbar. ''Son of a—!'' Reacting on pure surprise and policeman's instinct, he reached for his Beretta, but ended up fumbling frozen-fingered with his zipped-up parka. Forget it. He had to settle for a scowl and a bark. ''Where did you get that?''

She stopped in front of him and raised the crowbar. He flinched, but she just showed it to him. ''This? Right behind me. It was leaning against the wall. I was bringing it to— You *are* scared of me, aren't you?''

It took a moment for his heartbeat and the adrenaline rush to subside, for her words to sink in. And for him to ignore them. ''Do you realize I could've shot you? Don't ever sneak up on me like that again.''

She gestured, waving the crowbar. ''Who's sneaking? I'm standing right in front of you.''

"Yeah, with a heavy metal weapon. Give me that damned thing before you—" Dan snatched the tool from her and, finally feeling in charge again, walked around the cabin to the bolted front door.

Joan was on his heels. "Why didn't you just shoot the lock off like they do in the movies?"

Dan sighed. "*A*—this isn't a movie. *B*—there's no props guy to bring me more bullets when mine are gone. *C*—we may need them all before we get out of here. And *D*—I would've done that if I hadn't found this tool."

From behind him came, "If who hadn't found it?"

Dan ignored her in favor of wedging one end of the crowbar through the padlock's loop. He then threaded it halfway through, gripped both ends and twisted viciously. The lock's metal snapped with a cold clunk. He lifted the padlock free of the staple, swung the hinged clasp away and pushed open the cabin's rough-cut wooden door.

The interior was dim, the air stale and cold, but it felt like home. Dan tossed the broken padlock onto a table and took stock of the one room. A wood-burning stove, a fireplace, a box of kindling wood next to it. Two sets of skis, an old metal-framed bed. A crude kitchen, including a sink and curtain-covered shelves, which would hopefully yield some canned goods. And—hallelujah—a two-way radio.

But before he could take two steps inside, and again from behind him came, "Admit it. You're afraid of me."

Dan pivoted to face his tormentor. "Look, I've added a crowbar to my arsenal. I'm cold. Tired. Hungry. And sore as hell. Let's not play 'Who's afraid of the big, bad convict' again, okay?"

She shrugged. "Okay. But you are. You wouldn't use a bullet on the lock because you think you'll need them all for me."

Dan nodded. "Keep reminding me. Now close the door.

I'll get a fire going while you see what you can scrounge up. Maybe some dry clothes, some food, hopefully. Whatever we can use.''

He fully expected her to argue, but surprisingly she just nodded and went to close the door. Next, she set about rummaging through the curtained shelves, as ordered. Dan watched her a moment, realized he was grinning at her, and then knelt in front of the fireplace. He dragged the wood box closer, searched through it. Kindling, logs, old newspaper, matches. Everything they needed.

Everything they *needed.* The two of them. Dan looked over his shoulder, stole a glance at Joan O'Leary. Turned profile to him, her long, red ponytail a soppy mess, the parka big enough for two women her size, she was sniffing and reading a can label. She looked terrible and cute as hell, all at the same time. Again and unbidden, a grin claimed his mouth.

Perhaps she felt the weight of his stare. Or perhaps it was just chance. But either way, she looked up at him. ''Do you like—?'' Her eyes widened, no doubt with surprise to see him grinning and staring at her. ''What?''

Down on one knee, his elbow resting atop it, Dan sobered, and said, ''Nothing. What were you going to say?''

Now it was she who stared at him. She then studied the can, and glanced at him again with those big eyes. ''I was going to say ravioli. Is that okay?''

Dan nodded, wondered at his thudding heart. She was so damned little and wide-eyed. Could she be as innocent, in all ways, as she looked? And why was he wondering that? And what had she just asked him? Frowning now, he tried, ''Yeah, that's fine?''

She held the can up for him to see. ''Good. There're two of them—cans of ravioli. And a can opener. And a pot. I'll...just heat them.''

Dan nodded, wished he could get over the urge to hug her to him and kiss her hair and tell her it was going to be okay. "Good."

She blinked, lowered the can she held. "What's wrong with you?"

Dan jerked and turned away, busying his hands with the kindling and his brain with words. "Nothing. I'll get this fire going and then we can heat that up. I'm starved, but all I want right now is warmth and dry clothes. How about you?"

"No kidding." Her voice fairly bubbled. Dan glanced over at her. She was grinning and saying, "Getting out of these wet ones will be a slice of heaven. I'd be happy just to wrap up naked in a blanket and get in that bed." Then her eyes widened and she wheeled to face the sink, showing him her back.

Dan watched her, considered her words. And her own reaction to her words. Chuckling, he went back to building the fire. Throwing a log onto the grate, he mumbled to himself, "I think you're afraid of *me*, Joan O'Leary."

5

"TELL ME AGAIN why I'm handcuffed to this bed." For effect, Joan rattled her wrist irons against the metal rung of the headboard. Sitting cross-legged atop the thick mattress on the unmade bed and wrapped in a quilt, she watched Dan scoot sideways on the spindly chair until he faced her. When he did, she added, "I told you I don't want to wear them anymore."

"Precautionary measure. And you'll wear them until I say differently. Now be quiet while I try to get this radio working." He turned back to the prehistoric-looking set and began twisting knobs and eliciting ear-splitting frequencies.

Joan grimaced at the noise and watched him. What choice did she have? There was no TV, no electricity, no regular radio. Heck, there wasn't even another room. Nothing but her and the deputy in a snowed-in cabin somewhere in the mountains. Under other circumstances, this could really be romantic. She glanced at the handcuffs binding her to the bedstead. Yeah, right.

Just then, Dan tensed, sat rigidly over the old radio. Joan sat up straighter, too, realized she was holding her breath. He'd gotten through. She listened in, heard him talking to someone named Cal, to whom he gave a bunch of coordinates regarding their location. Done with that, the decipherable part of the conversation began.

"Good to hear your voice, too. No lie. I thought we were corpses. What? No, the Cessna's taking a dirt nap at the bottom of the mountain. It won't be hard to spot when the weather clears." He listened and then said, "We're fine. Yep, we both made it. Me and my prisoner." With those words, he turned and looked her in the eye. Joan held his gaze, even when he added to Cal, "Well, she *says* she did it. I guess I have to believe her."

Joan made a face at him. He chuckled and turned back to the radio set. But then his voice became strident. "What? Her apartment was ransacked? Interesting. Who'd you say was asking about her?" Again he turned to her. Joan's breath caught. There was only one person who had any reason to go through her stuff or to ask around about her. She raised her chin one defiant notch, watched Dan's expression harden. "Great. That's what we need."

Then he faced the set again, listened and said, "No, don't try to send anyone. It's too remote, and the weather's still unstable. Besides, with what you just told me, it might be best if we don't come down right now. What? Snake River Lodge? Good idea. I'll try tomorrow, if it quits snowing. I'll call you and let you know. Yeah, you, too—hey, Cal, you still there? Good. Um…is Lena still around? Oh. Well, I guess I deserve that. Then can I get you to swing by and check on Grandpa, tell him I'm okay?"

He turned again in his chair to face Joan as he signed off with Cal. "Yeah, that's it. Thanks. You're a good buddy, Cal. Remind me to buy you that beer I owe you. Yeah, thought that'd cheer you up. Okay. Talk to you tomorrow. Over and out." With that, he flipped a switch, the radio went dead and Dan lifted the headset off his ears, setting it on the table in front of him.

Then he draped an elbow over the chair's back and turned to her. The roar of silence rent the air between them. But finally, the deputy spoke. "Someone broke into your apartment and ransacked it. Seems too that your name's come up in Taos. Word got back to Cal that some bad guy was in town, asking after your whereabouts. What would you know about that?''

Joan's heart flopped around in her chest. ''Nothing.''

''Nothing?''

''Yeah.'' He wasn't buying it. She dropped it, asked a question of her own. ''Who's Cal?''

''A high-school friend. And a fellow deputy.''

She nodded. ''Oh.'' And asked her real question. ''Who's Lena?''

His expression closed. He raised an eyebrow. ''None of your business.''

Joan nodded her head, said, ''She sounds pretty.''

''She is.'' Dan then gave her a look that swung the conversation back to her business. ''Cal says this bad guy was seen in Taos around the time of the murder. Then he left and came back, hunted for you and now he's gone again. No one knows where. But talk has it that this guy killed Tony. So, my high-school chum says you're more a witness than a suspect.''

Joan eyed him right back. ''I think your high-school chum thinks too much.'' She tugged the quilt around her half-naked self and looked over at her drying jeans. Tossed over a chair, they roasted in front of the blazing fire in the grate. She swung her gaze back to the fully clothed deputy and felt at a disadvantage. Seeing him watching her every move, she said, ''Will you please see if my pants are dry? I'd like to put them back on. My legs are cold.''

He shook his head. ''They're not dry yet. I can see water still dripping off the hem. Just get another quilt.''

''Sure. Since I'm chained to the bed, I'll just drag it with me over to that linen chest right there by you.''

He narrowed his eyes at her. ''Why don't I hand you one? It'd be easier.''

"Thank you. And why am I handcuffed again? I've co-operated since you took me into your custody. I saved your life back at the airplane. I found this cabin and I heated up that ravioli for us. Yet this—'' she glared at him, rattling her manacles for emphasis ''—is the thanks I get. Why?''

"Because I say so." With that, he stood up and stretched. Despite being ticked at him, Joan caught her breath, watching the play of muscles under his knit shirt and shoulder holster. She flicked her gaze to his face. The tired lines, and maybe a few worry lines she saw there, melted her heart. Poor guy. He yawned and rubbed at his jaw. She really should go easy on—

He waved a hand at her, ordering, "Get up."

Sympathy died as Joan arched an eyebrow at such an imperious command. *I don't think so.* She stayed where she was, watching him lift the lid on the linen chest and grab two heavy quilts. Tucking them under his arm, he came toward her. He handed her a blanket, then again waved that hand and ordered, "Get up."

When he stood expectantly in front of her, Joan lost her defiant nerve and, clutching her quilts around herself, scooted off the bed. She then stood to one side as best she could, given the turning radius of her handcuffed arm. "What are you going to do?"

He looked surprised by her question. "I'm going to go to sleep. It's been a long day and I'm beat."

"What about me?"

"What about you?"

"Where am I going to sleep?"

He looked from her…to the bed…and back to her. "Right here, I guess."

"I don't think so."

He shrugged his broad shoulders. "Suit yourself." And climbed onto the squeaky-hinged bed. He rolled to the far side, against the wall, and stretched out, flipping his quilt over himself. Then he rested his hands atop his chest…and closed his eyes. Joan huffed out her breath as forcefully, as loudly as possible. He opened his eyes and rolled his head until he looked into her eyes. "What?"

"We cannot both sleep on this one bed."

He sighed audibly and raised onto an elbow. "Under normal circumstances, I would be a gentleman and agree with you. But this is survival, Joan. Nothing less. We're snowed in. We've been in a plane crash. And lived. What are the odds? I don't think it'll kill us to sleep in the same bed for one night. Do you?"

Well, that was entirely logical. But standing there in her underwear and socks, a T-shirt and a couple of ratty quilts, she didn't feel logical. The very idea of…*sleeping* with him. "Uncuff me."

He shook his head. "No." Then he lay back down, snuggling under his quilt and closing his eyes.

"I can't sleep like this." She rattled her chains to define *like this.* "My arm will get numb. And I can't even turn over. I like to sleep on my stomach."

"Too bad. Now lie down. I could use your body heat."

Outrage forced a snort out of her. "Use your own body heat."

Dan opened his eyes to narrowed slits. "This is not a battle you can win. Yes, there's just you and me and one bed. But trust me, this whole day wasn't one big scheme to get you into it. We're here, and if we want to keep warm, we'll have to sleep together. So, lie down. Or stand there and do whatever it is you're going to do. Because I'm going to sleep." Having said that, he resettled himself and closed his eyes.

Curling her lip, Joan mouthed, *Because I'm going to sleep,* and then plopped down as heavily as she could onto

the mattress, making sure she made the springs squeak and
the whole bed shake as she twisted and turned, faking settling down. Without warning, without opening his eyes or
even raising up, Dan clamped his hand over her quilt-
covered chest. "Knock it off."

Joan knocked it off. Wide-eyed, she stared up at the cob-
web-draped, rough-cut ceiling rafters. After a moment, Dan
slid his hand away. Joan lay beside him, aware of his
weight next to her, his heat warming her, his nearness com-
forting her. And couldn't stand it. "I can't straighten my
quilt over my legs."

"Dammit." Dan sat straight up. He wrenched her quilts
from around her, neatly flipping her over onto her side and
twisting her handcuffed arm. Squawking out her protest,
mortified that her bottom was now greeting him, Joan
flipped back over in time to have the deputy cover her with
the quilt and stuff it all around her from neck to toes.
"There," he said, looming over her. "Anything else, Your
Highness?"

Joan's jaw jutted out. *The big jerk.* "Yeah. Can I have
a drink of water?"

He glared down at her. "Go to sleep."

SOMEWHERE IN THE NIGHT, a powerful urge to sneeze
wrenched Joan from sleep. Lying on her back, she helplessly sucked in a huge breath at the instant she awakened,
and all but doubled over when her screechingly loud
"Achoo!" reverberated throughout the cabin.

Before she could blink, before the sneeze was an echo,
she was smashed under Dan's weight and had a faceful of
his gleaming eyes and his gun. Joan's muscles seized up,
her jaw dropped. Fright tap-danced over her nerves.

"What the hell are you doing?" His voice sounded gritty

with sleep. But his grip on her and the feel of the gun's cold steel against her cheek were anything but drowsy.

Cringing, she squeaked out, "I sneezed. As in achoo. You know, bless you, *Gesundheit*?"

He stared into her eyes another long, cold-steel moment, and then finally relaxed. But only enough to slide his weapon away from her and allow Joan to catch a gulping breath. She sucked in air to her grateful lungs. "Get off me. I can't breathe. You're too heavy."

"Am I? You really want me to get off you?" he said without moving off her. His expression warmed up, heating her through to her bones. Joan stilled in his embrace, blinked up at him, felt a growing tightness in her chest and also…somewhat lower down. "You haven't answered me, Joan."

"I know," she breathed, wrestling instead with what was going on inside her head. What was this instant attraction between them? She'd felt it from the moment he'd walked through the door of Interview Room 3. And now, why'd he look so darned right, here in bed with her? Did some parts of her know something they hadn't told the other parts?

"Is that your answer?" Dan all but whispered, his eyelids drooping sexily, his lips parting, his head lowering to hers.

"I guess," she murmured, raising her head and slanting her lips toward his. At the moment of sweet, firm contact, electricity crackled across her mouth, took her breath. A guttural noise escaped Dan. He gathered her into his arms. Joan melted against him.

His plundering tongue hungrily took her mouth. Joan heard her own whimper. She wanted this. Didn't want to think about how wrong it might be, just how good it felt. Breathing shallowly, she fisted her free hand in his black hair. He tasted good...so right. She couldn't remember the last time a kiss had actually made her hurt. Or feel so...alive.

Dan slid his mouth off hers, traced kissing nips down her cheek, her jaw and then her neck. Joan felt the cold air caressing her damp mouth. She arched into the deputy, then cried out when her arm cramped. He pulled back abruptly, stared wide-eyed down at her. Joan stared up at the fire-shadowed planes of his face. Then, she stretched her arm out, causing the handcuff to clink against the iron headboard.

And that sound, more than the one she'd made, acted on Dan like a cannon shot. He looked down at what he...they were doing, and instantly rolled off her. For her part, Joan lay absolutely still, having no idea what she was supposed to think, much less do. From his side of the narrow bed came, "I told you not to make any sudden moves."

"What?" The word was a cry of protest. A taut jerk of her head and she was facing him. "All I did was sneeze. You're the one who—"

He reared up on his elbow again. "I know what I did. Just go to sleep."

Joan clamped her lips together and glared at him. Finally, Dan lowered himself to the mattress and stretched out. His shifting about and settling in rocked every spring the ancient bed possessed. Joan clutched at the old ticking, held tight, feared she'd end up dumped on the floor. But finally he settled in, stilled. The room quieted.

After long moments, Joan stole a glance his way. His eyes were closed. She shifted her position to see him better. The man was handsome. And some kisser, for a deputy sheriff. But more than that, he wanted to help her, was going to help her. Why? He didn't know anything about her, but it didn't seem to matter. So, what manner of man was he that he'd risk his life to help her—a stranger and a convict? Well, a nice man, that's what. A caring man. A man of honor and scruples.

And armed with a 9-mm Beretta. But sound-asleep. Joan inched her hand over to him, aiming for his belt loop, for the metal ring that held the keys to her handcuffs.

WHEN DAN AWAKENED the next morning, the only thing remaining in the bed with him was his own handcuffs. They dangled, like a taunt, from the iron bar to which he'd fastened them yesterday. *Son of a*— He jerked upright, aware of the cold bed, the colder cabin and the dead ashes of the fire.

The day's achingly bright sunshine streaming in through the window over the bed pointed out the lack of drying clothes over the chair and the lack of their owner on the premises. Instantly gone from his mind was any memory of her rounded little bottom stuck up against his groin for more than half the night. Only an embedded sense of decency, and a severe grip on his pillow, had kept him from—

"Oh, just shoot me now," Dan appealed as he took inventory of himself. Beretta still holstered. Checked his jeans' pockets. Everything in there. Belt loop…key ring…*dammit*…gone. Prisoner gone. Cessna gone. Career gone. So escaping was how she paid back his many kindnesses, not the least of which was his intention to save her from herself? His jaw set with rage, Dan kicked free of his tangled quilt and scooted off the bed.

In a flash, he'd shrugged into his parka and was lacing his boots. She couldn't have gotten far. Not in this snow and cold. He tried to tell himself he worried only because she was the state's property and his responsibility, but he couldn't even sell that to himself. Damn her. She'd get herself killed, that's what. If he had a lick of sense, he'd leave the misguided little nutcase out there to freeze to death.

Yeah, yeah, Hendricks, tell it to someone who'll believe it. Ignoring his morning bladder, Dan jerked open the cabin door. Stopping short, he raised a hand to shield his eyes as he blinked against the stark white of the landscape. Polar-bear-in-a-snowstorm white. Rubbing away the tears, he blinked again and looked around.

"Dan? Oh, thank God. Over here. Hurry."

Dan heard Joan's frantic whispery call and wondered when he'd become Dan to her. But couldn't see her. He looked to his left, to his right, all around. She wasn't anywhere he could see. Refusing to admit he was the least bit spooked, he reached for his gun. "Where are you? What's wrong?"

"Shh. Keep your voice down. Just come here. Over to your left."

Palming his gun, he looked to his left. Lots of trees. No Joan. "If this is some kind of a trick, I'll—"

"There's no trick. Just hurry."

She sounded increasingly desperate. Leading with his weapon, Dan set out toward the trees. Just as he passed a particularly gnarled-up pine trunk, he heard a hissing sound above him. In less than a second, his attention and the 9-mm were aimed at the sound. Finally, what exactly he was looking at registered.

Joan O'Leary, confessed murderess and escaped convict, straddled a high-up thick branch and was hugging the trunk. Dan didn't know whether to laugh or cry, so he settled for calling out, "How in the—?"

"Get up here. Hurry. Bears in the outhouse."

"What?" He holstered the Beretta and put his hands to

his waist. "Did you say you were bare in the outhouse? It's kind of cold for—"

"Not me. Last night, you were asleep and I had to go…potty. So I took the key to the handcuffs. And then again this morning, I— If you'll come up here, I'll explain."

Dan couldn't believe this. She'd done it again—stolen official police property. Just like she'd tried to do in Houston with that officer's gun. He shook his head, but to keep from chuckling. "I'm not going up there."

She shrugged her shoulders. "Suit yourself. But there's a mama bear and two babies coming up behind you."

"Uh-huh. Sure there is. Go on."

"Okay. But don't say I didn't warn you. Anyway, I got up this morning and *dressed,* thank you, and went outside. I was in the outhouse when I heard a noise." Something behind him distracted her momentarily, but then she refocused on him. "There really are bears. Do you think that I'd be sitting up here on this branch otherwise?"

"That's another thing…how *did* you get up there?"

"Very quickly, that's how."

He nodded, quirked his mouth. "Because of the bears, right? You're going to have to do better than that."

"Well, I'm sorry, I can't. It's the truth."

"Somewhat like your confession?"

She eased her two-handed grip on the trunk enough to lean over and send her cascade of long red hair falling forward. "If I were you, I wouldn't split hairs right now. You're in a lot of danger."

Dan realized he was enjoying bantering with this good-looking crazy woman up a tree. "From who—you? I've got the gun."

She shoved her hair out of her face and held it back. "You may need it. Because coming up behind you is a nursery rhyme turned ugly."

"The Three Bears, I take it?" Dan grinned at her. "Does that make you Goldilocks?"

Joan started to say something, but swallowed the words and stared without blinking when, from behind him, came rooting and snuffling and grunting. Dan tensed. He stared up at Joan. Saw the bulge of her eyes. Knew he was in trouble. Before anyone could say, "Who's been sleeping in my bed?" he'd skinned up the tree, forcing her to scoot backward on the branch, and sat perched next to her. Only then did he look down.

Sure enough, a mother grizzly and her two good-size cubs ambled from behind the cabin and into the clearing around it. Dan's heart nearly tripped over itself. He turned to Joan and whispered, "Why didn't you tell me there really were bears down there? I could've been killed."

Disbelief shaded her green eyes. "I ought to push you out of this tree."

"Just try it." Dan kept his gaze on the grizzlies, saw the big, brown mother become aware of them. Across the way, the hairy critter raised on her back legs and sniffed the air. Dan clutched at Joan's parka-covered sleeve. "Don't move," he whispered. "But be ready to jump. Bears can climb trees."

Her inhaled breath was a mere hiss. "My, aren't they clever?"

Dan spared her a glance but reserved his undivided attention for the heavyweight mama now directly below them. Just as the grizzly shuffled up to the tree's base, her cubs got into a rolling ball of a squabble, bleating their displeasure with each other. Mother Bear turned and, with an indifferent swipe of a massive paw, separated them. Undaunted, the cubs scrambled to all fours and followed their mother's ambling gait into the open front door of the cabin.

Oh, hell. No one had to tell Dan what the next words

out of his prisoner's mouth would be. He glanced at her. Sure enough, "Don't look at me. You were the last one out, Sheriff."

He wasn't taking this lying down…or sitting in a tree. "Only because I had to come find you."

She pointed a finger, opened her mouth, but got distracted, along with him, by the unmistakable sounds of the cabin being vandalized as only three hungry bears can do it. After a sickening there-goes-the-food moment, Dan exchanged a look with Joan. She immediately quipped, "It's not like we have to eat every day, I guess."

He nodded, trying his best not to appear as though he was staring into her green eyes and remembering their kiss. "Good thing," he finally thought to say by way of a response.

She stared back, her expression warm. Then she looked down and away, and chuckled, swinging her gaze back to his face. "So, Sheriff, do you go out on a limb like this for all the girls?"

Dan's eyebrows veed toward his nose. "No. Just the ones charged with a capital crime and being chased by bears."

Joan's expression crumpled some. But she gamely raised a hand, as if to identify herself at a roll call. "Here, sir. Joan O'Leary, president of that club."

Dan quirked his mouth, chiding himself for having brought that up. Not that it was a big secret, but still…he'd really killed the moment. Then he heard that thought. *The moment? What moment?* That did it. There was no moment. She was his prisoner. Dan got them both back on track with a sober expression. "Tell me about you and Tony LoBianco."

JOAN FROZE at his words. She gripped the branch's rough bark, shifting from one increasingly numb butt-cheek to the other, before countering with, "First tell me about Lena."

The deputy eyed her but then, surprisingly, told her about Lena. "Lena's my girlfriend. Or was."

Her heart leaped, unexplainably, at his word choice. "Was? Sounds ominous." So why was she so happy about that?

He shrugged. "Could be. Probably is ominous."

What woman in her right mind would leave this man? He was handsome, accomplished, intelligent, funny—*Joan, get a grip.* "Um, probably?"

His frown stayed in place. "You're on some pretty personal ground here."

"Look again, Sheriff," she teased. "We're not on any ground here."

Dan shot her a sidelong glance and said, "Fair enough. Okay, she wanted to get married. And I have no idea in hell why I'm telling you this."

Joan ignored his disclaimer in favor of commenting, "A problem with commitment?"

The man narrowed his eyes at her—a clear warning she understood but didn't heed. She shrugged. "I thought we'd bonded after our crash, that it gave me the right to poke my nose into your business."

"Well, it doesn't."

"Sorry." The moment stretched, the cold invaded her bones, her belly rumbled its hunger. Seeking to amuse herself—they *were* still sitting out on a limb in the frozen badlands of New Mexico—she ventured another question. "So, how long had you and Lena been girlfriend and boyfriend before she popped the question?"

He stared at her—overly long, in Joan's opinion—before saying, "Three years." He managed to sound as if she'd dragged it out of him with forceps.

"Three *years?*"

His expression became pinched. "I don't have a problem with commitment."

Joan pulled back, stared. "Tell that to ex-girlfriend Lena."

"This conversation is over." He frowned down to his ankles to prove it.

Joan huffed out a breath. "Okay. So, do you want to watch some TV?"

He stared at her for a long time. "I get it. We're stuck in a tree with nothing else to do but talk, right?"

"Right. One more question?"

Dan scrubbed a hand over his face and jaw. "All right, but make it true-false, please. No more essay."

"Fine. When you were talking with Cal, you asked if Lena's still around. So, I'm guessing she ran out on you, right?"

Dan gave her a look that most people reserve for those individuals they don't like a whole lot. "True. You happy now?"

Strangely enough, she realized, she was. But she opted for discretion over valor. "Is your butt numb? Mine sure is. And this branch isn't getting any softer." She shifted her weight, crying out when she nearly unseated herself.

Dan grabbed her arm to steady her. "Easy." Then he surprised her by going *way out* on a conversational limb. "About last night...that kiss? I shouldn't have done that."

Joan looked into the warm light of his hazel-green eyes and prayed he couldn't hear her heart hammering away. "Well, it's not like I didn't kiss you back. So, no big deal."

"Yeah, it was. I know better than to do something like that. You're in my custody. I ought to be more...detached, I guess."

It was Joan's turn to drop her gaze to her dangling legs.

In the ensuing quiet, she could hear the bears having a smorgasbord of destructive fun inside the cabin. But suddenly she couldn't keep her thoughts to herself. She turned to him and blurted, "So why aren't you? Detached, I mean. Somehow, I don't think you've had this problem before. And I mean that kiss, not the plane crash."

Dan surprised her with a look that mingled guilt with shyness. "You're right. I haven't had this problem before. And why aren't I detached? I can't tell you. Probably something to do with you, wouldn't you say?"

Joan's eyebrows raised right along with her heart rate. "Could be. I guess we have to make sure it doesn't happen again."

He continued to stare at her. "Yeah. We sure do."

Huffing out a heated breath, Joan leaped into neutral territory. "So, tell me about Grandpa. You asked Cal to check on him."

"You're a good listener, aren't you?" He contemplated her a moment and then cleared his throat. "Okay. About Grandpa. But I still don't have any idea why I'm telling you all this."

Joan shrugged at the mystery of why he was, too. "Maybe it'll be good for you. Who knows?"

"So now you're playing therapist, huh? Well, anyway, the old guy's more my father than his own son's ever been. I think he tries to make up for him. Long story short, he lives with me." He then shook his head and chuckled. "How many people do you know whose grandfathers get named in paternity suits?"

Joan hit at him, nearly unseating them both. "Get out! You're lying! A paternity suit? How old is he?"

Dan frowned in thought, crinkling the skin at the corners of his eyes. "I'm thirty-two. My father, then, is fifty-four. So…Grandpa is seventy-six." He looked as surprised as she felt. "The old guy is seventy-six, and he's making babies—allegedly. The expectant mother is a forty-five-year-old woman who works at the hospital. Guess who's not allowed to, um, *volunteer* there anymore? And guess why?"

Joan shook her head. "I don't need to. But he sounds great, like someone I could hang out with. And probably would. So, look at you—you'll have an infant aunt or uncle."

He laughed out loud, which made her grin, and said, "I guess so. I hadn't thought about that."

His laughter had a way of finding her heart, making it thump. She couldn't look away. A shallow breath helped her croak out, "Any brothers and sisters?"

Still chuckling, he added, "Older sister. Kim. She and her family live in Santa Fe, close to my mother. And I have a half brother somewhere."

"Somewhere? So, you don't get to see him?"

Dan looked away, got quiet and concentrated on the snowcapped mountains in the distance. "No. I was eighteen when my father left—the last time. He remarried, had another son. Brent. He's eleven years old now."

Joan wanted to touch him, to comfort him. Somehow, his hurting seemed to be her problem, too. But all she could do was sit there, knowing she didn't have the right to comfort him. Instead, she chirped, "Are you a native of Taos?"

He swung his gaze back to her. "Yep. Lived here except for college and those five years on the Houston P.D."

She nodded at his answer. "So why'd you move back to Taos?"

His somber quiet deepened. Then Joan remembered—his wife. She also remembered that he didn't know she knew about that. Sergeant Mackleman got those thanks. But again, Dan's loss seemed the same as hers. As if her losing her parents, and him his wife, gave them a past together. Maybe that was why she was swallowing a wad of tears, wanting to hold him and to keep him from further hurt. So she said, "I'm sorry if I've stepped over some line—"

"No, it's okay. I moved back here for lots of reasons. The main one, I guess, is my grandfather. Even though he doesn't believe it or act it, he's getting older and needs help. But before that, my...." He stopped, looked away, but then turned to her. "Never mind. It's not important."

But Joan knew it was, knew what he'd been going to say. About his wife. Sympathy squeezed her heart. But she said nothing. What could she say?

Dan took another breath and added, "Let's just say Houston lost its charm. Then, Ben Halverson called me about a job opening, asked if I wanted it. So here I am." After another moment of quiet, he eyed her. Here it came, she knew. The hot seat. Sure enough, he said "Tell me about you. Help me understand the life you're so willing to give up for Tony LoBianco."

6

DAN'S WORDS reminded Joan of the cold, of the rough bark of the branch under her. She shrugged, quirked her mouth. "There isn't much to tell. I don't know my real family. I'm told my mom was a kid herself and alone. She abandoned me twenty-eight years ago, when I was a baby. It was probably the only thing she could do. So the great state of Texas raised me in foster homes."

Dan's expression softened. Apparently it was his turn to feel sorry for her. Joan hated this part. Always the sympathetic look, the poor-baby stuff. But Dan surprised her, and warmed her grateful heart, with a matter-of-fact question. "So what was that like? The foster homes."

"It wasn't horrible," Joan heard herself going on. "I was taken out of a couple places where the people were into foster care for the money. But then I got placed, when I was ten, with Bob and Pam Jackson in Houston and got to stay there. They're great people. I love them like they're my parents. In fact, I tried to reach them when I was...there, but I...well, they weren't home. I'm kind of worried, too. They should've been there. And I know they've seen all this on the news by now. I can only imagine what they must think."

Dan sent her a sincere smile and said, "When we reconnect with civilization, I'll call Hale and Carter, ask them to send someone around to check on them and anyone else you're concerned about."

Joan's whole spirit brightened. "Thanks. That's really nice of you."

He grinned, ducked his head. "We cops have our moments, too."

Joan laughed, then told him, "I have two friends, Brenda Martin and Kate Jefferson, who might know where Bob and Pam are. Maybe Hale and Carter could call them."

"Okay. Just remind me of the names later. So, go on. What about the rest of your life?"

Joan stared at Dan. Where had this great guy been when she wasn't charged with a capital crime? Seeing him raise an eyebrow, and realizing it was because she was staring, Joan said, "Oh. Um, when I was eighteen, I started college and put myself through with a job in a tag agency and some scholarships. Got my degree. Moved out. Dated. Lived my life. Screwed everything up over a man. And here I am. End of story."

"Well, not quite the end. But let's talk about that man you screwed up your life with. Tell me about Tony Lo-Bianco."

Joan's breath caught. Tony LoBianco wasn't who she'd meant. Jack the ex-boyfriend/ski instructor was. Now what? "So, what do you want to know?" she squeaked out.

"The truth would be nice," he said…pointedly. "Because once Ursa Major and The Minors clear out of the cabin, you and I have work to do. We'll clean up the mess and then I'll write the owner a note. And—"

Joan cut her gaze to the cabin. *Come on, Mama Bear and Baby Bears. Show yourselves. Help me out here.* She focused again on Dan. "A note? To explain all this destruction?"

"Yeah. And about who to contact for reimbursement for the damage and for the things we're going to take."

Good. Keep talking about this. Anything but Tony Lo-Bianco. "What are we taking? And why?"

He pinched his face up, adequately expressing his desire not to be questioned. "The why is because we're leaving. And the what are things like gloves, scarves and goggles. Then I'll radio Cal and we're outta here."

"Where're we going? Snake River Lodge?"

"Snake Riv—" He gave her a look of chagrin.

Joan quirked her lips. "It's a small cabin. I couldn't help but overhear."

"Uh-huh. We're going to the Taos Ski Valley. Not too far from here."

"Sounds wonderful. As long as I don't have to ski. Wait. Why would a *ski* lodge be open in September?"

Dan cocked his head, looking at her as if she were a demented person whose medication had worn off prematurely. "Why? Because tourists happen. People come up here to hike, get away from it all. Take in the scenery. And to get snowed in and wear orange parkas. Like us."

She wrinkled her nose at that. "So I'm supposed to schlepp over this mountain—me and my tennis shoes? Great. I ought to have a full-blown case of pneumonia by this afternoon."

"No schlepping. We're skiing. There are two pair in the cabin."

"And one will stay. I do not ski."

He huffed out his breath. "Joan, watch my mouth move. We're skiing."

She watched his mouth move, liked it a lot, heaved out a breath—and then shook her head no. "No, *we're* not. I can't ski. I won't."

"Yes *we* are, and you will. So get ready for a crash course—no pun intended. Because we can't stay here."

"Why can't we? I like it here. It's nice."

Now Dan huffed out his breath. "Not anymore it isn't. Because *A*—the supplies are low, and will be much lower when our furry friends are done. *B*—there's more weather on the way. See those dark clouds building up over that range? *C*—there's no easy way to get rescued here. And *D*—"

"Just cut to *X, Y, Z,* please."

He narrowed his eyes at her. "And *Z*—now that Mama Bear knows there's easy food here, she and her cubs will be back as regularly as poor cousins."

As if on cue, the threesome in question waddled fatly out of the cabin's front door. Trailing behind them were shredded quilts and the litter of the cabin's entire contents. Joan's heart sank. She watched their Wild Kingdom visitors until they disappeared into the thick undergrowth across the clearing. She listened until their snorts could no longer be heard.

Only then did she exchange a look with the deputy out on the limb with her. "So! We're going to ski, huh? I've always wanted to learn how."

"THIS IS NOT GOING to work. It's impossible. You're going to get me killed."

"Have I yet?" Tying a rope around Joan's waist while she held her arms out to her sides, Dan raised an eyebrow at her.

His red-haired prisoner huffed out her obviously low opinion of his guardianship over her life. "No, but not for lack of trying. Let's see, there was the snowstorm, the plane wreck and the bears, to name a few. Do you always lead such a life of adventure, Sheriff?"

"Deputy. And no, I don't. Lead a life of adventure, that is." With that, Dan stepped back and surveyed his handiwork, adjusted the knot, tugged on the rope looped around her parka-thickened waist. He then squatted to check her tennis shoes' fit in the toe bindings of the old cross-country skis from the cabin.

Fiddling with the adjustments, he divided his attention between the skis and her face. "And just for the record, this crazy stuff never happened to me before I hooked up with *you*. So maybe you're causing it."

He stood up, watched Joan's narrowed so-green eyes sparkling with confusion. She shook her head. "You're laying all this at my door? I'm the boring accountant. You're the dashing cop-slash-pilot. All I want in my life is stability. Maybe a husband and kids. The house with the white picket fence. You know, the American Dream."

Dan chuckled, trying not to look at her pink and pouting mouth, only inches away. "*A*—there's not the least thing dashing about me. And *B*—if you want to live the American Dream, don't go around killing mobsters." With that, he looped his fingers through the rope around her middle and gently tugged her forward, toward him. "Good advice, no?"

Slip-sliding on her skis, nearly losing her balance, she screeched and grabbed for his arms, holding on. "Don't let go! I'm liable to rocket down this mountain, doing about ninety miles an hour with no way of stopping. And pinging like a human pinball off every tree and boulder— What's so funny?"

"You," he didn't mind telling her around his chuckles. "I am in over my head. No doubt about it." Then, gripping her elbow to steady her, he reached over to retrieve two ski poles from where they leaned against the outside wall of the cabin. He staked them, one to either side of her, in the hard-packed snow and said, "Here, hold on to these so you don't jet down the mountain."

Grim and silent, she clutched at the poles and stared up

at him. Dan stepped back, advising, "Go on, work with them. Get used to their feel. And be careful of the pointy ends."

"Oh, even better. I'll fall and shish-kebab myself."

Dan watched her awkward efforts, thinking she looked as though she'd sprouted a few extra limbs. But when she finally seemed to have the hang of the poles, he sidestepped her and started to crunch his snowy way toward his skis. Another grin lit his face. He realized he was trying to picture his cool, blond, take-control Lena in this situation. Couldn't do it.

Wait a minute—she was no longer *his* Lena. Dan stopped in his tracks. Lena was gone. Just up and left Taos, heading back to San Diego. Shouldn't he be crushed? Or guilty that he wasn't? He frowned, assessed his feelings, realized he was neither. So, Lena was right—he didn't love her. But he should've. She was perfect for him. Intelligent, warm, loving. Self-contained, successful, a real adult.

But what he'd really liked about her, came the unguarded thought, was that she could take care of herself. She didn't really need him. Dan stiffened, as if someone had put a gun to his back. That department shrink in Houston was right. So was Joan. He didn't want to commit, to be needed. Because of Marilyn? The truth now blinded him, like the sunlight glinting off the snow. All these years after her death, and here he was…still protecting his heart, still refusing to feel. Still throwing himself into his work, avoiding finding anyone to care about again.

When are you going to accept that Marilyn was taken from you, killed in a stupid, senseless crime? A drunk driver, Dan. Not you. It wasn't your fault. Maybe not. But it felt like his fault because here he was, a cop, and he couldn't even protect his own wife, hadn't been there when she'd needed him the most. Dan narrowed his eyes, looking around and wondering why he was thinking about this. He hadn't dragged this baggage out in years. So why now?

An alarmed yelp from Joan had him jerking around. *Look at her. With all that flailing about she's doing, in about a half second, she'll be on her butt.* Shaking his head, glad to be out of his thoughts, Dan sprinted forward and put out a hand to steady her. "Whoa. Easy does it. Don't fight them."

"Give me your gun, and I'll show you a fair fight, Sheriff," she snapped.

Dan chuckled. "I'll pass. Here, like this." He adjusted her hold, showed her the desired motions. "See? Don't make it so hard."

Within seconds, she smoothed out her motions and raised a happy face to him. "Look at me—I'm skiing!"

Again Dan laughed at her. "I'll be the judge." He continued to watch her, telling himself he needed to make sure she got her legs under her. But his subconscious knew better. *What did you feel when you kissed her last night? Was it real? It was, wasn't it? Come on, buddy, give her a chance.*

Again Joan bleated out her alarm. Again Dan rushed to steady her, to touch her…liking the feel of her too damned much. And why did he? She was exasperating, frustrating, infuriating. He bit back a grin. And funny, charming, intelligent. Scared, brave, sarcastic. All that and more. *Admit it. She excites the hell out of you. What you feel is passion. Passion for her. And passionately about her. In other words, you care, Dan. A lot.*

"Sheriff, you're in la-la land. Why are you staring at me like that?"

Dan jerked back to the moment. "Was I staring?"

"Yeah. Like I'm something really yummy on a stick." With that, she went back to her ski-pole maneuverings.

But Dan's attention remained riveted on her. He surprised himself with the realization that he didn't particularly like liking her. If he stuck around, if he helped her as he'd said he would, she'd make him care about someone again, he could just feel it. She'd make him risk it all, make him hurt again. Why? Because she needed him? Or was it that he needed her...needed her zaniness, her fighting spirit and sheer pluck, even in the face of such desperate odds?

Dan sobered even more, stared at Joan's now-thoughtful expression as it rested on him, and saw something meaningful reflected in those green eyes. It staggered him, forced him to brace his knees or fall to them in the snow. What if he couldn't save her? What if she was convicted, and the state administered a lethal injection to put her to death? Bile rose to the back of his throat. No, forget this—he couldn't afford to care. Refused to.

And so he said, "Let's get on the road." With that, he turned and made his way over to the other pair of skis. With the practiced ease of years of skiing experience, he strapped himself onto them. And denied that he burned with an anger that he couldn't name, an anger that he couldn't direct to the guilty person. Because he didn't know who it was. Her or himself.

He forced a coolness he didn't feel into his words. "Where we're going, there're other people. You're still under a warrant. So, once we're there, I'm duty bound to keep you cuffed and separated from the population. Understand?"

"Yes," she said from behind him. "I'm not to forget who I am, who you are, or why we're here. Or there. As if I could." A moment later, though, she called his name. "Dan? After Snake River, what's going to happen to me?"

Dan clenched his jaw, bit back a curse he wanted to yell at the world for putting him here. Still down on one knee, he looked over his shoulder, sought her gaze. Saw the uncertain puckering of that bottom lip, the vulnerable tilt of her eyes. His heart lurched. *Dammit.* Again anger welled up in him. This time, it had her name on it. How dare she light a spark in him, threaten his world, and then not do a damned thing to help herself—or allow him to help her? He stood up and turned expertly on his skis to face her.

Hands to his waist, he repeated, "What's going to happen? The same things that would've happened without the snow or the crash, Joan. When the weather clears and the roads are passable, we go down to Taos. And then I turn you over to the state for prosecution. And possibly execution."

Her expression crumpled. Good. No doubt his raw assessment hit home. She lowered her gaze, stared at her ski blades.

Dan's hands fisted so tightly, they hurt. He wanted to shake her until she cried, until she hurt the way he did, until he'd wrenched the truth out of her. Almost afraid of what he might be capable of, so strongly did he feel right now, he took several deep, calming breaths. Only when he felt more in control did he say, "Joan, look at me, please."

She raised her head, gave it a toss to flip her ponytail back over her shoulder. And then silently stared at him, waiting. How should he put this? "No games here, no lies. It's just you and me. I want the truth. Did you kill Tony LoBianco? I can't believe I'm going to say this, but yes or no—either way—I can help you. I *will* help you. Either way."

Joan took a breath. Blinked. Looked haunted. And then said, "And that's the part I don't get. Why should you help me? What's in it for you?"

Dan turned his cold face up to the bruised sky, dark with snow clouds. His chest hurt from her question. What was in it for him? This was too raw, too strong, too real. He didn't want to feel this. Then, fine. He heaved out his breath and looked back at her, shrugging. "Nothing's in it for me. Forget it. Can't say I didn't try."

With that, he grabbed the loose end of the rope tied around her and fastened it around himself. He felt her gaze on his face but refused to look at her until they were tied together and it was time for his final instructions. When he did meet her gaze, his heart lurched yet again. Her green eyes were dull with mistrust. He pretended not to notice. "There's no way in hell this is going to work—and I mean our skiing in tandem like this—but we don't have much choice. You ready?"

Frowning, her bottom lip puckered, she nodded. "As I'll ever be."

So HE HAD TO STAND her on her feet again, Joan fumed. So he again had to adjust the rope that bound them together. So? She watched Dan sidestep in his skis as he once again—okay, the tenth time since they'd left the cabin four hours ago—left her standing there and crabbed his way back down the mountainside. She could hear him mimicking her. Did he think she was deaf?

"I told you I'm ready. Of course I'm ready. Why wouldn't I be ready?" His singsong voice accompanied each angry step. "Ready as I'll ever be, she says. Ha. How about not at all ready, not in this lifetime?"

"I can hear you," she called to his retreating back. "I told you I can't ski. Is it my fault it's taken us four hours to go about ten feet? I can't help running into you and knocking you down. Whose idea was it for you to tie this rope between us anyway—" She stopped when he whipped around to look at her.

Almost at the end of their shared rope, he pointedly staked his poles in the snow and glared up at her.

Joan returned his look. Not that he could see much of her expression. He'd tied her parka hood so tight that she had to look out at the world through a tiny little gathered circle that revealed only those features right in the middle of her face. Two beady, goggle-covered eyes, the tip of her nose and barely a lip.

"Be quiet and let's get moving, Joan. I'm waiting."

And you can wait until hell freezes over. She considered her icy surroundings and amended, *And you can wait until pigs fly.* Who'd he think he was, giving her a direct order? As if she'd just salute and obey. So there she stood, wobbling unsteadily and windmilling her arms in an effort to keep her precarious balance. She raised a covert eyebrow and silently dared him to come up here and make her do as he said.

"If I come up there, it'll be to untie you and leave you here."

"I should be so lucky," she yelled. Dan made a move toward her. Joan...well, changed her mind about cooperating and squatted in a crouch atop her skis. She grabbed at the umbilical-cord rope connecting her to him. And then bounced a bit until she felt her weight was distributed and she had her balance. "Okay, let's go. I'm ready!"

Dan nodded that he'd heard her and muttered, "I've heard this before." Then, with practiced grace, he turned to face the trail he was blazing. One mighty shove and they were off—yet again. Dan grimaced as the rope around his waist pulled taut against the drag of Joan's body at the other end. If she had her eyes closed again when he needed to stop, like the last time...

Why would she close her eyes? Look at this scenery. Sliding past them was a tranquil winter wonderland of packed snow and white-dusted pines. Then suddenly, Dan realized, they were doing it—they were skiing in tandem. Hey, this wasn't so bad. Pretty smooth, even. So why couldn't they have done this four hours ago, before Agony of Defeat Mishap 769 during which she actually lost her ski poles?

It was his fault she'd lost them, just ask her. He was the one, she insisted, who'd sent her poles airborne off that cliff and made her lose them. Only to have them rain back down, like knitting needles, and narrowly miss pinning them to the earth. As if that wasn't enough, she was still defending herself regarding that whole incident involving the nonexistent mountain goats.

Just then, in the present, and right in his path—much to his frozen, teeth-chattering horror—a jagged ledge of rock loomed. *Oh, hell.* He didn't have time to go around it. He had to stop. *Joan, I hope you're paying attention.* Dan swung to the right, knees bent, skis dug in, and slid to a picture-perfect stop about two feet from the ramplike ledge of rock. He huffed out a relieved breath. Too soon. Joan squawked out a warning. His legs spread, Dan pivoted to see what... *Oh no.* She was going to...ski right between his legs. If he was lucky.

At the last second, Dan leaped to one side and hit the ground hard, eating snow. A split second later, Joan came hurtling and screaming right past him. When the rope binding them snapped taut, she came to an abrupt halt and collapsed to the ground.

A moment of silence was observed before Dan jumped up and pitched a cursing fit as he wrenched himself free of his skis. Then he was standing over Joan. She lay on her side, looking stunned. She blinked repeatedly and stared at...nothing. Dan huffed out a white cloud of breath. *Dammit.* His anger—as always in the face of her willingness to follow his lead, no matter how dumb the idea turned out to be—evaporated. Cursing himself now, he bent over her, grabbed her by the parka and wrenched her to her feet…well, her skis. Or tried to. Too many moving parts. It was like unfolding a stubborn lawn chair.

Then, spitting, blinking, wiping the snow off her goggle lenses with her mittened hands, Joan gained her balance and—Dan sighed—began griping. "This is not working. It's like trying to ski down a giant waffle iron. We have been introduced to every log, stump, exposed rock or antlered creature for miles around. Just end this torture—toss me off the side of the mountain."

Dan brushed at her, too, trying to help, but getting mad again. "What do you think I've been trying to do? I have *never* seen anybody so uncoordinated."

"I told you I couldn't ski. I wasn't lying." She smacked his hands away.

"It's hard to tell with you."

"Ha, ha. Look, I'm fully prepared to sit right here and die. I'm soaked through. I feel like a swizzle stick in a frozen drink. So I'm not going another step…or skip…or slide, or whatever it is you do on skis."

"*You* don't do a damned thing on skis."

"Is that not what I've been saying, beginning with when we were sitting up in that tree? Now, I propose I save New Mexico a bunch of time and money and just end it right here. I don't even care, at this point."

"Well, dammit, I do."

She stilled, cocked her head and roved her gaze over his face. "You do?"

Suddenly he was sure that he did, on some level that had nothing to do with official duties or that woman-in-jeopardy thing the department shrink warned him against. "Yes," he said truthfully. But then he lied about the reasons. "The countywide elections are in full swing and Ben Halverson is up for reelection. He can win, too—if he doesn't get hung first because we can't solve the LoBianco murder. So, yeah, I care.''

Her expression changed, hardened, closed off. ''How selfish of me. Had I known, I would've killed Mr. LoBianco sooner, turned myself in and made you guys heroes. And just eliminated that whole campaigning phase for you.''

Dan's expression hardened right along with hers. ''A word of advice here. If you're going to stick to your I-killed-my-lover story, you ought to drop the 'Mr. LoBianco' and call him Tony. That would make it a *little* more believable.''

Joan leaned toward him. ''Go to hell, Sheriff.''

''For the last time, I'm a deputy, not the sheriff. And I'm beginning to think this—right here with you—*is* hell.'' With that, he grabbed the rope around her waist and began unknotting it, not caring if he jerked her around.

''What are you doing?'' Joan shoved against his hands and then his chest.

As solid as the mountain behind him, Dan ignored her protests and kept working, freeing first her then himself from the rope. Only then did he square his jaw and say through clenched teeth, ''Quit shoving me or I'll fashion a noose out of this rope and loop it over the nearest branch.''

''I dare you,'' Joan taunted. And then gasped when he gripped the rope in both hands. But he just tossed it to the ground and bent over to unbuckle her from her skis. Half expecting her to clobber him while he was down there, Dan hurried his hands and straightened up. Without a word passing between them, he grabbed her parka at the shoulder seam and plucked her off the misused blades.

Then he wrenched his goggles up, hoping the heat of anger he still felt blazed from his eyes. ''I've had it. I'm ready to duke it out with you right here. I was going to wait until we got to Snake River, but forget that. It's here and now. We're putting the gloves on. So get ready to rumble."

Through the tint of her goggles, he could see Joan looking at his gloved hands and then her own sopping-wet mittens, and then again at him. "Has your brain frozen solid?"

"Probably. But we're still going to have it out."

She raised her goggles, the better to show him her own glare. "Fine, but I get equalizers—like some rocks and a big stick. And no fair pulling your gun."

Puzzlement had him frowning. "What? I'm talking about answers, Joan. Truthful answers. Right here, right now."

"Answers? Well...whew! I thought you meant we were going *mano a mano*. But...too bad, because I don't feel like talking right here in the great outdoors. And you can't make me."

Dan jutted his jaw out dangerously. "Try me."

Joan's bottom lip poked out. She looked him up and down. Dan couldn't believe it. Was she actually considering trying him? But then she slumped, and grumped. "Fine. So, do you think I just got up one day and decided to confess to a murder? No, I didn't. Things happened. I didn't ask for it. And you don't need it. So, forget it—I won't involve you."

One giant step had him up close and holding her by the arms. "Look at me. I'm involved up to my eyeballs. I don't need you to protect me. I chose to place myself in danger, and I chose to pursue the truth. So get real. And quit trying to be so noble."

"Noble? Me?" The red in her cheeks deepened. She wrenched out of his grasp. "I don't think so. And how do I get real, Dan? Tell me how."

"I can and I will. But you make sure you want to hear

it. Because, like it or not—and I know I don't—there's
something here between us. You've got my attention, okay?
Like no one and nothing has in the past five years. And I,
for one, intend to find out exactly why that is."

Joan blinked. "Man, you are some piece of work, Sheriff. Okay, it's not getting any warmer, so I'll bite. Tell me
what you think it is between us."

He looked into her eyes, deepening the quiet around
them. Then he ran a hand over his mouth. "It's physical.
And strong. But more than that…I don't know what. I just
know we have something between us. Can you feel it?
Right here?" He poked a finger against her parka-covered
chest, right over her heart.

Joan looked down at his finger against her chest. Her
defenses tumbled like wooden blocks. What he was sug-
gesting—that he felt something for her, something strong
enough to warrant discussion right here in the waning,
freezing daylight—caused emotion to well up in Joan like
rising mercury. She fought tears as she looked at him. "I
do. But I can't, Dan, not where I'm going. Don't ask me
to feel this now."

"I didn't ask." He removed a glove and rubbed his hand
over his beard-stubbled jaw. "And you can, Joan. You can
feel. You don't have to throw your life away like this. Hale,
Carter, even Mackleman told me how they tried to help
you, tried to get you to talk to them, to trust them. But you
wouldn't. And now you won't let me in. Why?"

Joan stood mute for long seconds, concentrating only on
her heart's increased cadence and trying to find the right
words. But Dan beat her to it. "Look at me, Joan." She
did. He firmed his lips and then said, "If you've never
listened to anybody before in your life, listen to me now.
You are safe with me. Don't shut me out. If you do, you
could very well lose your life."

Joan wanted to run from the fear, from the truth…into his arms. But she didn't move, only fisted her hands. "What you don't understand is, either way, guilty or innocent, I stand to lose my life, Dan."

He threw his hands up and raised his voice. "How can being innocent cost you your life? I don't get that. Just like I don't get how you can be so willing to trust your fate to a faceless legal system, but not to me. I'm part of that system, and I'm standing right here in front of you, Joan. And telling you I care. Doesn't that mean anything to you?"

Joan frowned, unable to speak, unable to answer him. Because she didn't know how.

Dan sighed out his breath and pressed his point. "Do you even know what I'm talking about? I'm not talking about a legal defense. I'm talking about you and me. Us. Whenever I look at you, I…dammit, I believe again. I begin to hope. That sounds crazy, doesn't it?"

Tears rolled down Joan's cheeks. Why now, with her life in a shambles? Why'd he come along now? "Stop it, Dan. Please. It's too late. I can't do this."

His expression spoke of his struggle to find the right words. "Do what, Joan? What do you think I'm asking you to do?"

Joan swallowed the lump in her throat. "I'm…I'm not sure."

He grinned…almost. "I didn't think you did. Yeah, I'm asking you to trust me, maybe let yourself care—about yourself, if not about me. I can live with that. But what I can't live with is not knowing, Joan. Not exploring this thing between us, this thing that makes me want to grab you to me and—" He bit back his words, his body jerking as if agitated beyond control. Then he went on. "It goes beyond the physical, but it's also gut-wrenchingly physical, in my chest, my heart. I don't know what it is. I—''

"Dan," Joan blurted out, cutting off his words. "It's okay. I feel it, too. I know what you mean. I just can't believe our timing. And I don't mean that we're freezing to death out here. I mean all of it. Me. This murder. That kiss last night. I thought I'd die, it was so…wonderful. Just…what do we do about it? I'd…" Her voice trailed off, the words she wanted to say too fragile for utterance.

Dan's hazel eyes lit with an intense emotion. "Joan, before we go any further, I want to tell you something, so you'll understand me better. It's about a woman in my past who needed me very much. She was killed by a drunk driver. The guy was a repeat offender wrongly let go by a glitch in the very system you want to trust your life to. I was a Houston cop then and got the call to work the scene—before anyone knew it was her. My wife. Marilyn. We'd been married six months."

Joan gripped his sleeve. "Dan, I'm so sorry. Sergeant Mackleman said something offhand about that, but nothing…no details."

A stark emotion ravaged his face, creased his forehead. But he went on. "Details. They were pure hell. I never allowed myself to *feel* after that—not even for Lena. Not deeply. Until now. Until you." His expression shifted, became quizzical, as if he struggled to figure out why that was. Then he smiled, saying, "I'm standing here like a big jerk, freezing my butt off, trying to say I want to try, Joan. How crazy is that? I want to try because, God knows, when I look into your eyes, I see a chance to be happy again, to *feel* something. But I can't, if you won't let me in, let me help you. That decision has to come from you."

Joan wanted to sit in the snow and cry her eyes out. How beautiful was this guy? He'd just said everything she could

ever want to hear him say. And here she had to tell him
no. For his own safety. "Dan, I can't. You can't. You'd
lose everything. Maybe even your life."

"Why will I lose my life, Joan? What's going on?
What's the truth?"

7

"THE TRUTH." What Dan asked of her held Joan frozen in place, as much as the surrounding snow and ice did. Yet inside, she burned with the truth, with what she suspected she felt for him. "What if the truth is that you can't help me? What then? What's that going to do to you? And to me, knowing how you'd hurt because of it? I can't do that to you. I won't."

Dan put his hands to his waist, looked to the ground and shook his head. Then he met her gaze, showing her an agonizingly serious expression. "Try me. I'm a big boy. Let me worry about me. Just tell me what's going on."

Joan stared at him. And saw her answer in the way he held his ground, in his dark eyes, in his hands to his waist. Her heart threatened to pound right out of her chest and kill her before she could get the words out. So, she took a deep breath and a big plunge. "All right. I didn't kill Tony LoBianco. I saw him being killed, but not who did it. Not the killer's face. I couldn't identify him. All I saw was a tattoo on his arm. Of a native chieftain in a feathered headdress. And now, I think that man is trying to kill me. That's why I turned myself in and said I did it."

Dan hadn't said one word while she spoke. Hadn't moved at all. And now, he still didn't. He just stared at her. Joan felt sure her blood was congealing as she waited for him to speak. Finally, he did blink. And then he muttered something, perhaps a curse, which she didn't catch because he swiped a hand over his mouth at the same time. Then he shook his head, looking at her as if he'd caught her stealing money out of his wallet.

Then he exhaled, shook his head. "I *knew* it. Joan, this scares the hell out of me. This is the *mob* we're talking about here. They're not known for forgiveness. They'll just keep coming, one after the other until you're—" He shut up and stared hard at her. "Your life is in serious danger."

Joan's heart lurched for a beat or two. "I know. That was made clear by two attempts on my life in Houston. Which is why I made up that confession. Getting myself thrown in jail was the only way I knew to put myself out of their reach. All I could do was pray for your investigation to point you to that tattooed man. Or for him to make a mistake and get caught."

Dan's deepening frown notched vertical lines between his eyebrows. He looked up and away from her, as if filtering and ordering his thoughts. After a moment, he sought her gaze. "Yep—panic-thinking. Probably even seemed like a good idea at the time. But you keep saying you trust the legal system. So why didn't you run to us, instead of away from us? We could've protected you."

"How?"

"Are you kidding—with all our resources? Believe me, we'd bend over backward keeping you safe. You're an invaluable eyewitness."

"No, I'm not. My testimony is worthless, remember? I didn't see his face. There's no way I could identify him. The back office was shadowed and smoky. And I walked right into the middle of everything. I saw this other man stabbing Mr. LoBianco. I was so shocked I screamed. And there I was, spotlighted under a bare bulb right inside the doorway. The killer turned and saw me. Mr. LoBianco was already on the floor, and the guy lunged toward me. I dropped the books and got the heck out of Dodge.''

Dan shook his head, looked very worried. ''Are you sure you didn't see anything other than that tattoo? Describe the guy to me. What he wore, how tall, things like that.''

Joan concentrated on calling up that night, and then spoke as the scene played again in her head. ''Not very tall. Husky build. Dark clothes. A hat, like gangsters wear in the old movies.'' Then hearing herself, she slumped. ''Sounds made up, like a movie, right? How could I go to the police with that? A tattoo and no face.''

Dan nodded, his expression thoughtful, assessing. ''Actually, that's a lot. You should've come to us.''

''And said what? Oh, hello, I just saw Tony LoBianco being killed by some stocky, tattooed guy in dark clothes, but I can't identify him. And oh, by the way, I'm his accountant and was taking the books to him with my questions about why things didn't add up.''

Dan grinned, giving it a fatalistic twist. ''I see your point. We'd have gone to the club, seen him stabbed—not a mob-style killing—decided you had opportunity. A motive would be easy to figure. And we would've arrested you.''

''And never looked for Tattoo Man, right? At least the way I did it, stupid and panicked as it was, it aroused your suspicions.''

''You're right. It makes dumb-luck sense. It also makes me cringe to think how wrong it all could've gone. And still could. God knows how many others are out there. And we don't know where.''

Dan rubbed his gloved hands up and down her parka-covered arms and spared her an apologetic smile. ''Right now, I want nothing more than to grab you and explore this whatever-it-is between us. But you're not safe, and that eats at my gut. And worse, the only way I can go about securing your safety is to place you in more danger.''

"Great," Joan muttered, frowning at him.

Dan grinned, rather sickly, in her estimation, and nodded. "Yeah, isn't it? But it can't be helped. The only way to catch this guy before he finds you is to get back in touch with the world, give his description to Cal and get started hunting for him."

Joan's fears rushed out with her cold exhalation. "Oh, Dan, do you know how much that thought scares me? If something should happen to you because of me, I'd just—''

"Shh. Nothing's going to happen to me. But if it did, it wouldn't be because of you. Don't forget that I wear a badge, that I took the oath that goes with it. So even if I didn't…have feelings for you, it would still be my job to protect you, at any cost. So there, it's out of your hands."

Joan felt the tears come to her eyes. She blinked them back and mumbled, "That doesn't make it any easier."

Dan tipped her chin up until she looked into his eyes, so hazel-green and warm with an unnamed emotion. Darn him. Even with his cheeks and nose red from the cold, with the goggles pushed up on his forehead, and his parka's hood framing his face, Dan had never looked more handsome. Her fluttering belly seconded that emotion. "Nothing easy was ever worth fighting for, Joan."

"Which explains us arguing all the time, I guess."

Dan chuckled and slipped his hands under her heavy coat to encircle her waist. "No, that's sexual tension that makes us fight."

Joan's heart pounded, her eyes widened, her cheeks heated, as did other areas…a lot lower down. She swallowed, clutched his sleeves. "I think what makes us fight is *not* doing anything about that tension, don't you?"

"Oh, baby," Dan breathed, exhaling a warm breath that

clouded the air between them, and slid his hands up her rib cage. "I think you're dead-on with that. When we get to that lodge and thaw out—and providing no vital body parts fall off—I'm willing to give you ample opportunity to demonstrate that alleged passionate nature of yours."

Joan pulled back in mock insult. "Alleged? Why, Sheriff, I'm guilty as charged on that crime. Now kiss me—hard."

ABOUT FIVE MINUTES LATER, Joan stood in front of Dan while he knelt on one knee and buckled himself onto his skis. Hands to her waist, feigning a frown, she watched him and teased, "You want *me* to climb on *your* back? Are you sure? I mean, I haven't consulted a how-to manual in years, but I think you have the positions reversed. For this to work, I need to be—"

"You need to quit talking dirty to me, is what you need to do." With his gaze still on his task, Dan shook his head. "Keep it up and I'll have a…third ski pole to deal with. Like I need the aggravation." Now he stood up, brushing the snow off his hands. "Piggybacking down to the lodge will look stupid. But it's that or walk. Or knock ourselves senseless and freeze to death. So while we're still young, just climb on and wrap your legs…" His sudden pained look said he had a mental picture going.

Joan bit down on the inside of her cheek until she was sure she wouldn't laugh. Served him right for bringing up that whole sexual-tension discussion. Now that she knew he felt the same way about her, that he had trouble keeping his hands off her, too, just as she did him, then it would be no holds barred from here on out. She'd show him passionate nature. Alleged? Ha. Time to separate the men from the boys. "So, Sheriff, I wrap my legs around your waist, and we…? Go on, I'm listening."

Dan exhaled hard enough to puff his breath into a good-size cloud. Again he tried. "You climb on me and wrap your legs around my waist…and…" Again his voice trailed off.

All serious business now, Joan nodded. "I got that part. My legs around your waist. And then what?"

Dan half turned, pointing distractedly in the direction that led down the mountain. "We ski down this mountain with you…like that. You on my back, your legs…" He gave her a look of sheer pain.

But now Joan had her own problems. All that piggyback talk had a painful ache centering itself…where it counted. She closed her eyes, shook her head, opened her eyes. Saw Dan looking at her mouth. She took a deep breath and huffed out, "Okay."

Dan repeated, "Okay." And stood there.

Joan took several lung-freezing breaths and prayed for detachment. When all she wanted to do was jump on him, wrap her legs around his waist—from the front—kiss him long and deep and—

Dan cleared his throat. Joan jerked her gaze back to his face. He'd stepped up to her, was right in front of her now, looming larger than life in her vision. She nearly sank to her knees. Did the man never quit? He had a dark, earthy sensuality about him that deepened with every self-assured movement, every pointed look, every heated word. "Climb onto me and hold on."

Joan's mittened fingers went to her mouth. She bit down on them and whimpered.

"Just climb on," he said huskily, turning his broad back to her and hunkering down, which tightened his denims over his heavily muscled thighs. She stared at them until she realized he was holding his hands up and out, ready to help her on, to steady her, if need be.

Taking a deep breath, but thinking she'd be better off to sit in the snow and allow it to cool the heat down there, Joan stifled a groan and gingerly draped herself over his back. Oh, yes. Hard. Muscled. Broad. Powerful. A moan of want threatened at the back of her throat. Joan bit at her bottom lip, and wrapped her arms loosely around his neck. Then, with a finality born of physical hurt, she lifted her legs, one at a time, wrapping them around his waist. And knew she was lost. Completely and totally.

But Dan stood up easily, as if her added weight were no more than a child's. He looped his gloved hands under her thighs and hefted her weight until it apparently felt balanced to him. "All settled?"

In an agony of desire, Joan nodded, realized he couldn't see that, and croaked out, "Yes."

Turning his head, as if to look over his shoulder at her, but with his face blocked from her view by his parka's attached hood, he said, "You'll be fine as long as you don't let go of me."

"I'm not letting go of you until you beg me to, Sheriff. I've been wanting to get a hold of you since you opened that door into Interview Room 3. And the feeling is just getting stronger with each passing minute."

Dan tensed, made a sound. A noise. A guttural, animal noise that Joan wanted to hear again. But as each agonizingly long moment passed, he didn't make that or any other sound. Nor did he move. He didn't say anything, either. But a series of exhaled vaporish clouds marked his breathing, confirmed he was still alive. Then, his voice a low, husky drawl that crept on kitty feet over her skin, he said, "That's deputy to you. And remember, I still have the handcuffs. If you don't behave, I'll put you back in them."

She grinned, glad he couldn't see her face. Inching up

his back some, she aimed for his ear, saying, "Is that a promise…Deputy?" She tightened her legs around his waist. "I'm going to hold you to that."

LATE THAT SNOWY AFTERNOON, Dan's imaginative but straining efforts paid off. He crested a bunny-course hill and sidled to a stop, staking his poles. Then he stared quietly, as if at a religious vision. There it was, laid out below him. The nestled-against-a-mountainside, wood-deck-skirted, shopping-center-and-nightclub-encircled tourist enclave. And all of it, according to the posted signs, Closed For The Season.

His heart sank. But then he saw the lights of the lodge itself, the shadows of folks moving around inside. Such relief swept him that he almost wept. The lighted sanctuary he'd sought all day. The brand new Snake River Ski Lodge of the Taos Ski Valley. Yes! Warmth, food, water, shower, rest. Joan off his back. Bed. Sleep. Call Cal and clear up this whole mess. And then get on with life. And Joan.

"Wow. This place is great," Joan the Igor-hump on his back chirped. "Look. We've been seen. We must look pretty funny to those people standing up there."

Dan nodded and shoved forward, perhaps a trifle too enthusiastically. Because in mere seconds, they were hurtling downhill, approaching warp speed. Joan gasped her alarm and tightened her grip around his neck. Dan gritted his teeth, wishing she'd not choke him every time she moved. Lucky for her that relief was at hand. Or would be, if only he could stop. Preferably before they got smacked, like bugs on a windshield, into the looming-ever-larger white fence around the ski lift's base.

The escalating pitch of Joan's screams in his ear kept Dan apprised of how close they were getting. Accompanying her aria was the Greek chorus of shouts from the folks pressed against the deck railing and gesturing madly for him to turn aside. As if he didn't know that. Still, Dan finally won some purchase on the icy hill and careened to a last-second, knees-bent, feet-pigeon-toed, skis-crossed stop.

In the blessedly silent aftermath, Dan remembered to exhale. He staked his poles, registered that his arms and legs felt rubbery, and his back was killing him. He bent forward, wheezing in and out. A buzz of excited chatter seemed to be getting closer, so he glanced in that direction. An apparent rescue team—four bundled grandpa-types—cautiously edged their way through the drifts. From the deck, the ladies called out for them to be careful. Dan then focused on his own problem, flinging two words over his shoulder to it. Her. "Get. Off."

"Oh. Sorry." Joan pulled and clutched and slid and climbed down him, somewhat as she had that gnarly-trunked pine tree back at Cabin Rustica. How many years ago had that been? Still hanging on to him—as if he'd been on her back and *she* needed steadying—she worked her way around him, raised her goggles and asked, "Are you all right?"

Trying to stay upright and at the same time breathe in and breathe out—in the correct sequence—he spent long moments staring at her. Only when he remembered how, did he nod and answer her. "I've. Been. Better."

She grimaced her sympathy and patted his sleeve. "Poor baby. Was I too heavy?"

Dan was not so tired and frozen that he'd forgotten his lines. "No."

She smiled. "Good. Stay right here. Some nice people are coming to help us."

Within minutes, those nice people—a handful of old-folk guests and a couple of young male lodge employees that

Dan didn't recognize—had him un-skied, and him and Joan inside, shed out of their wet outer clothes, cuddled together on one of the lobby's big, overstuffed sofas in front of the roaring fire in the grate, blankets wrapped around them and warm rum-laced toddies cupped in their hands. And fielding about fifty thousand questions.

None of which Dan got to answer, seeing as how Joan beat him to the punch every time and had their geriatric audience enthralled with her lies. Yes. Lies. Every one of her answers. The why of her lies eluded him. What was wrong with the truth? He thought about that. Oh, yeah. Bloody murder. Capital crime. Prisoner. These sweet old people would flee like frightened deer. So Dan relaxed some, listening in on Joan's rendition of their lives.

Well, relaxed was a relative term, lasting only until she said to Gertrude Binder, a white-haired, cherubic older woman who inquired about their marital status, "We're newlyweds from South Bend, Indiana."

We are? Dan lowered his mug to his lap and stared hard at Joan. Then he scanned their attentive grandparental audience. Yeah, they liked the idea of newlyweds. Great. Now all he needed was for some of them to be from—

"Why, me and the wife are from South Bend," chimed in a short, thin old guy with a graying mustache. "Lived there all our lives. Well, not all our lives—not yet, anyway. Right, Mother? Ha, ha."

Ha, ha. Great. Dan took a sip of his toddy, electing now to stare straight ahead. No way was he getting drawn into a conversation about landmarks in that fair city, one to which he'd never been. South Bend? Where the hell had she pulled that city from?

"Oh, you are?" Joan gushed to the friendly gentleman. "Why, we might know some of the same people. You'll have to talk to my husband about that."

Dan swallowed his sip in a gulp, scalding his throat. "I don't think—"

"Oh, do that later," said a pleasingly plump matron with big, jet-black-dyed hair. Dan could have kissed her for saving him like that. She turned to Joan. "So are you kids on your honeymoon?"

Here we go, he thought fatalistically.

Sure enough, Joan took to that idea like a petty thief to a convenience store. "Why, yes, we are. How'd you guess?" She grabbed Dan's arm to prove it, and turned a lovey-dovey expression up to him.

He managed a grin for the round of congratulations coming their way and then eyed his "wife," giving her his best you-can-stop-anytime-now look.

Of course, she didn't. But looking down into that pixie face—one he suspected he'd want to wake up to and see every morning for the rest of his life—was Dan's further undoing. He was in over his head. It was that simple. One little green-eyed, red-haired woman and he was sunk like a submarine. All he could do was sit and watch her—and listen very closely to her lies so he'd know what their story was. In case anyone should ask him.

Right now she was regaling their elderly audience with the tale of how they came to be stranded here. *This ought to be good,* Dan thought as he tuned in. "We were driving through to...Tucson when the snow hit and stranded us in our car. It was awful. We just finally had to abandon our new...Corvette and ski out."

Tucson? Corvette? Dan's eyebrows slid right down over his nose as he again stared at her. He ought to ask her why they had skis and heavy clothes, since they were just driving through. In eighty-degree weather. In the valley. But he couldn't. He was, after all, a participant and, to all intents and purposes, had been there and lived that. It didn't matter, though, because he couldn't have found a conversational opening what with all the sympathetic tsk-tsking and hand-patting from the old folks clustered around him and his wife of ten seconds.

"I think the worst part was the bears," Joan explained, and Dan sputtered. She patted his knee, no doubt as a gesture of appeasement, and never missed a verbal beat. "They came right at us, all thr—five of them. Huge bears. Hungry bears. It was awful."

That elicited gasps and a breaking-up into discussion groups where everyone simultaneously recounted for his or her neighbor a personal encounter with bears. Dan took that opportunity to lean over and whisper, "Don't forget the plane wreck and how you're a murder suspect in my custody. Or do you think that'd be stretching it a bit?"

Joan patted his cheek and whispered, "Leave me alone. I'm on a roll."

"I see that. While you are, try coming up with something to tell Mark Jacobs—my *friend* and the manager of this place. But mostly, I'm wondering what your groupies make of my shoulder holster and the handcuffs dangling from my belt loop. Strange devices for a man on his honeymoon."

Joan eyed him and pursed her lips into a pout, speaking low and seductively. "Then again, maybe not, Sheriff."

Dan's breath caught. "Now see? It's that brilliance of yours—that's why I married you. I like how you think." With that, he straightened up and grinned behind his toddy mug, again content to let her bury them all in more lies.

Before she reconvened the nice old people around her, she arrowed him a long-lashed, sidelong and sexy pout, and then chirped, "Now where was I? Oh, I remember—the day before the snowstorm. I was so helpless. I mean, there I was…Dan had me handcuffed to that old metal bed and was getting ready to—"

Hot toddy spewed like sea spray from Dan's mouth as he pitched forward. Several hands attached to clucking voices reached to pound his back. Someone even raised Dan's arm over his head and shook it. When he could, Dan extricated himself from their helpful clutches and said tightly, "I'm okay. Thank you. Yes, I'm sure." Then he turned to Joan. "Sweetheart, I'm sure these folks don't want to hear the gory details of our—"

Several loud protests to the contrary from Joan's agog audience assured him that they did indeed want to hear the gory details. Dan shot his bright-eyed and grinning *bride* a warning look. And that was when big, blond Mark Jacobs walked up to the little group, recognized Dan and called out, "Hey, buddy, I had no idea—"

Dan's head-shaking and narrowed eyes stopped his friend's words and brought a frown to the man's face. Dan immediately stuck his hand out to Mark, saying, "How are you? Thank your staff for me for coming to our rescue. I'm…" *Who am I?* Had Joan told anyone their names, real or otherwise?

"Ken Thompson," she supplied, adding, "and I'm Barbie. Newlyweds from South Bend, Indiana."

Dan's eyes began to water. But he held his expression and Mark's gaze. By sheer dint of will. Mark stared at him, then at Dan's outstretched hand. After a moment, his expression cleared and he shook Dan's hand, saying, "Well, Ken and…Barbie, welcome. Let me tell you what everyone else knows. Snake River is a new lodge, so not all the rooms are ready yet. But we're pretty much stranded here—without our maids or our chef. We have plenty of food and drink. As well as warmth and company. So, everybody's pitching in, making do with what we have."

"Whatever you can do, we appreciate," Dan assured

him, looking his friend directly in the eye and nodding while he spoke.

Mark nodded right back and handed Dan a room key. "All I have to offer is this room with a king-size bed. But since you're…newlyweds, that's probably fine, right?" He shot Dan a what-the-hell-is-going-on? look and added, "Once you're settled in, could I talk with you a minute in my office, Da—Ken?"

Da-Ken shoved forward on the sofa, grabbed his *wife's* arm and stood them both up. "Nothing would make me happier, Mark."

With that, and for some reason Dan couldn't immediately fathom, everyone was staring at him. Then he realized his gaffe. Mark had never said his name. Dan quickly searched his friend's shirtfront. No name tag. *Oh, hell.*

Joan…Barbie, bless her heart, pulled back some in his grip to look up at him. He telegraphed her an evil-eyed look, but it did no damned good. "How do you know his name?"

A waiting silence again occupied the next passing seconds. Dan seethed, wanting very much to kill her. Right there in front of everyone. But before he could do that, or come up with a statement appropriate to mixed company, Joan crumpled her expression and all but whispered, "Oh, no, it's happening again."

What is? was all Dan had time to wonder before Joan, appearing greatly upset, turned to the enthralled assemblage. "It's his psychic powers."

Dan gaped from her, to the wary old folks, to the struck-dumb Mark, and back to…Barbie for her explanation. He was not least among those wanting to hear this one. "Sometimes," she began, "after a lot of sex, the powers rekindle themselves, and Ken really can't control them.

Why, he's not even aware of what he's saying. He just blurts things.''

Dan blurted, ''What the hell are you talking about, Joan?''

''See what I mean?'' she deadpanned, shaking her head sadly, accepting the murmurs of sympathy coming her way. ''He calls me by other names,'' she stage-whispered. And further confided, ''Ignore it—and the cursing. And the gun—it's not loaded. He just likes to carry it. Not that he ever gets violent…as long as I'm with him. Don't talk to him if I'm not. Because I couldn't be responsible for what he might—''

''That's it.'' Dan's bellow had the old folks—and Mark, who should know better—gasping and jumping back. Dan shot them an irritated scowl and tightened his grip on Joan, too late directing her steps across the flagstoned floor of the lobby and away from her audience. He marched her directly toward the split-log stairs to one side of a small gift shop.

Once there, he turned to the wide-eyed assemblage across the way. ''We're very tired. We'll see you in the morning.'' Then he turned to Joan. ''Upstairs, Barbie.''

8

"KEN AND BARBIE? Thompson and Tucson? Our new Corvette? Where the hell did all that come from yesterday? And why?"

Joan signaled for him to hold on until she swallowed the last of her breakfast biscuit. Dan waited impatiently. When it was down, she complained, "Are we back to that? It's all you ranted about last night—before you fell asleep and snored all night, let me add. I told you already that I wanted, just once, to be a normal, happy family. I've never had that. I like that story better than—"

"Than what—the truth? You and your happy couple from South Bend. And normal? Who came off as normal—you? Certainly not me. Everyone here thinks I'm psycho." Dan looked her up and down, adding, "You're a pretty convincing liar, you know. Should I be concerned?"

With that, he got up from his chair at the doll-size table and loaded the meal's remains onto a tray from the lodge's kitchen. Joan grabbed for the last piece of bacon. She bit into it, chewing thoughtfully as she turned those baby-greens on him. "No cause for concern, Sheriff. I tell the truth all the time. Well, except for the past week. But these are pretty weird circumstances, you have to admit."

"I freely admit it. And they get weirder every time you open your mouth. Last night when I went down to get our supper trays, people scattered to the four winds."

Joan chuckled and waved the crisp bacon at him. "This

is good. Did Mrs. Binder fry it? Tell her how much I enjoyed it.''

''Yeah, yeah… Are you finished eating yet? I need to get going.'' Not waiting for an answer, he pulled her plate from in front of her and stacked it atop the other dishes already littering the tray.

Her frowning gaze followed his actions. ''Well, I guess I am.'' Then she turned her face up to him. ''Where are you going now? And why can't I go? I'm bored, Dan. I've had a bath, I've eaten—ta-da, day over. If the other guests don't see me soon, they'll think you did something to me and storm the room.''

''*A*—why would they do that when Mark has a key? But *B*—considering the ages of the other guests, I'd pay money to see that. Now come on, get up.'' He headed for the room's exit door and set the tray on a blond three-drawer chest next to it.

''I hate it when you do that *A, B, C* thing. And do you hear how you talk to me?'' she called to his back. ''You sound like you're talking to a dog. Or a trained seal.'' She huffed out a breath, heavy on the melodrama. ''I just don't see how this marriage can work. Father Evans tried to tell me. And Mother was right—I should've married Scott.''

He turned around. ''Stop that right now. None of those people exist.'' He glared a moment, bit back the question, refused to ask it, refused to play into her hands. But couldn't, for the life of him, stop himself. ''Who the hell is Scott?''

Her mouth turned down in petulance as she pulled herself to her feet. ''Wouldn't you like to know?'' She dragged her terry-robed, barefooted self over to the upholstered chair he'd positioned in front of the closet door last evening.

Watching her, noting every nuance of her being and her

bearing, and sighing over what he saw, Dan unsnapped the handcuffs from his belt loop and decided he hated them more than she did. But he couldn't yet give in to her moping and those big green eyes. He knew she was bored and resentful. But better those than dead. Which she could be if he let her roam freely and mingle. Because he hadn't yet checked out all the guests. No sense taking chances with her life. His chest tightened at just the thought of her in danger.

Dressed in his same clothes from yesterday, with his Beretta stuck in his waistband but hidden under his knit shirt, Dan approached his...what the heck was she? "Speaking of our *marriage,* we're stuck with that stupid newlyweds story, you do realize."

With her drying hair hanging loose all about her, making her look morning-decadent and warm-bed desirable, she flounced onto the chair, sitting heavily. "I know. But if last night was any indication, I'd still be a virgin."

Dan stopped right in front of her. "Time out. Whoa. A virgin?"

She looked up at him. "Huh?" Then hit at him. "No. Give me a break. I got over that years ago. I was just using it as an expression."

Dan nodded his relief. "Good. Virgins are too much trouble. Don't look at me like that. I'm thirty-two, not sixteen. And we were *both* worn-out last night, as I recall. A sandwich, a shower and sleep. That's all either of us could muster." He clicked the one cuff around her so-slender wrist. "And this morning, who was up and in the bathroom, the door locked, before I even rolled over?"

She pulled a face, admitting, "Me. I thought...well, I thought we were going to...you know. Remember our talk yesterday in the snow? About us?"

"Oh, yeah, I do." *Okay, now we're getting to it.* Dan

grinned as he looped the other cuff through the closet's brass hand-grip and locked it. Then he settled a stare on her that he hoped was at hot as he was beginning to feel. "So tell me, why'd you lock the bathroom door? I would've taken a shower with you."

Her face colored, but she raised her chin, telling him, "I didn't know that bathing prisoners was included in your job description. That would approach above-and-beyond, I'd think."

Dan leaned over her, bracing himself with his hands on the chair's armrests, and planted a smooching kiss on her lips. "With you, sweetheart, I'm fully prepared to go way above and beyond." Then he traced her lips with his tongue, sipping and swirling until she made the gasping sound he wanted to hear. He pulled back, sought her gaze.

Her kiss-wet mouth was open, her breathing shallow, her eyelids drooped heavily. "Not fair," she whispered, lifting her mouth for more.

"But a part of my charm, ma'am." He nipped biting kisses along her jaw, deftly avoiding her questing mouth. That was for later.

"Charm, huh? If you're so charming, how come you handcuffed me to this closet door? And how come you're leaving me…like this, hmm, Sheriff?"

"Oh, man," Dan breathed, allowing his head to hang limply down. "Whew. When'd it get so hot in here?" Then he straightened up…well, the parts of him that hadn't already…and told her. "Just hold that sprawled pose while I'm gone, okay? Because I can't…do this—" he looked down at himself and then up at her "—despite appearances, until I know you're safe here. I want to check the guest registry, see if I find anything suspicious. If the phones come on, I'll call the department, tell them what you told me and get them working on that angle. Then I'll be right back.''

''I hope so. I'd hate to have to gnaw my hand off at the wrist to get free.''

Dan chuckled. ''And I believe you would, too. But you won't have to. I'll be right back, especially with you looking like…you do now,'' he finished on a lame note, then cleared his throat, as if that would clear his head. ''I'll be right back.''

Joan nodded, puckered her lips at him and stretched like a lazy cat in the sunshine. ''You already said that, Sheriff.''

''Huh? Oh, I did. Right.'' Dan frowned. Where was he going? And why—with this female display right in front of him? It wouldn't come to him. ''Where was I going?''

''To the lobby. The guest register.'' Then she sat up straight, dropping her languid pose for a look of genuine concern. ''I drank a bunch of coffee. What if I have to go before you get back?''

Grateful for the head-clearing change in subject, Dan hitched his jeans around and reverted to his lawman demeanor. ''You just went. But cross your legs if you get the urge.''

She made a face and asked, ''What if there's a fire?''

''There won't be a fire.'' But thoroughly guilty now, Dan squatted in front of her, bracing his hands on the armrests. ''Look, when I get back, maybe we can go mingle some. There's a library–sitting room thing on the third floor where everyone gathers. We'll join them. How's that sound?''

That brightened her green eyes and warmed his heart. ''Great. And I want to eat lunch downstairs, too. I swear I won't…embellish our lives. Well, not any more than I have to, because of what I've already told them.''

Dan chuckled at her wide-eyed good spirits and wondered if he'd ever be able to tell her no and mean it. ''Okay, lunch. I'll give them our reservations." With that, Dan pushed himself to his feet and adopted a scowl. "For the record, Scott is scum. He'd never make you happy. Not like I can."

Grinning now, she challenged, "We'll see, won't we?" Then she dropped her gaze, as if suddenly shy, and softly asked, "Dan, while you're downstairs, can I get you to do something for me?"

Leaning over her, close enough to smell her hair, and with his hands again braced on the armrests, Dan planted a tender kiss on her forehead, her nose. "Name it."

"Good." She one-handedly pushed him away and became all female business. "Remember that lobby gift shop by the stairs?"

Too late wary, Dan straightened up. "Yeah. Why?"

"Well, I could really use some makeup. And something to read—a woman's magazine. Not that hunting or car stuff. Oh, and I need clean underwear, too—size 4. And warm socks. And remember that really cute sweater that was hanging in the window? The green and maroon and blue one, cable-knit, kind of bulky, with the little-children-of-the-world scenes knitted into it? Get that in a medium. And make sure the socks go with the sweater."

"Make sure the socks," he heard himself repeating and shut up, staring at her. "Anything else?"

She gave every appearance of thinking about it before pointing at him and blurting, "A candy bar. Anything chocolate—with nuts."

Dan nodded at this red-haired, green-eyed creature chained in his bedroom. What time was it when he lost control of her and the situation? "A candy bar, chocolate with nuts. I'm really scared to ask, but is *that* all?"

She shrugged. "For now. Oh, and if you have any money left over, get yourself something nice."

He nodded his head fatalistically. "Yeah. Thanks. I will."

"You will? What're you going to get? I may want some, too."

Dan grinned all over himself and tousled her hair. "You can have all you want, greedy. Trust me, I'm more than willing to share what I'm buying."

She cocked her head, her expression changing to curious. She couldn't stand it—he knew it. Sure enough, she blurted, "What're you getting?"

"A great big, brand-new, shiny box of…condoms." Her shocked gasp accompanied him as he strode away from her with an exaggerated swagger. When he got to the door and gripped the knob, Dan turned back to her, saw her reddened face and winked. Then he opened the door, peered into the narrow hallway, checking left and right. Deserted. Stepping out of the room, feeling smug, as though he'd gotten her that time, he started pulling the door closed behind himself.

"Dan?" Joan called out.

Somebody wants the last word. Grinning, he pushed the door open enough to allow for peering back into the blue-and-tan-wallpapered room. She'd stood up from the chair. He raised his eyebrows and said, "The name's Ken. But how can I help you?"

"Let me show you." Instantly, her expression became slinky, sensual. With her free hand she unknotted her robe and allowed it to gap open…just enough. She was naked underneath. Simpering like a silver-screen vamp, with her voice a husky, breathless whisper, she breathed, "Don't be gone long. Or I may be forced to take up with the first key-toting, sexy pilot-slash-sheriff named Dan to walk through that door."

A LITTLE WHILE LATER, Joan stopped in the act of crossing her legs when a key scraped in the lock. She stared at the door. *Tell me he forgot something. Because if this isn't Dan, I have to start gnawing.* The door jerked open and in strode Dan. Relief cut through her like a bolt of lightning. But it was short-lived, that relief was. Because the deputy didn't say a word to her. With only a dark-eyed stare directed her way, he closed the door behind him.

For her part, Joan stared back wide-eyed as he just stood there, clutching a bulging, white-plastic shopping bag that bore the lodge's gift-shop logo. What was wrong with him? Had he never seen a terry-robed woman chained in his bedroom before? Aha…there it is. She glanced down at her all-but-naked self. Lots of skin showing. It probably explained that intense, hot-eyed stare that heated her, like the fire in the grate.

Joan drifted her gaze over to the shopping bag that dangled from his left hand. She glanced back to his face and raised an eyebrow in question. He eyed her a moment longer before turning that same scrutiny on the bag, holding it up and out in front of him as if he had no idea how or when it became attached to him.

But he didn't fool her. She knew what was in that bag, what it was he wanted her to find. Just to prolong his agony, though, she purposely ignored it to ask, "Did you and Mark find anybody suspicious in the guest register?"

He never looked away. His hot, assessing eyes roved over her. "No. You're safe here."

Oh, so we don't like to talk when we're aroused. Joan tilted her head, causing her unbound hair to fall forward in a sensuous slide over her shoulder. "Good. I'm glad."

He nodded. "Me, too. But the phone lines are still down."

"Too bad." She expected him, at any moment, to jump on her, half wished he would. Then, affecting nonchalance, she finally nodded her chin toward the bag he held. "What you got there?"

A black eyebrow winged up. "Stuff."

"I bet." Joan bit back a grin and again purposely delayed him in his erotic mission. "You're breathing heavy, Sheriff. Did you knock yourself out getting back here so fast?"

"Do I look tired to you?"

Far from it, Joan thought and crossed her legs. Wantonly. With a lot of opening-of-the-robe over her bare thighs.

He noticed. And sucked all the air in the room right up through his flared nostrils. Then his tongue tipped out to wet his lips. He flicked his gaze back to her face. "What was the question?"

Poor baby. He was undone. But, excited by this highly charged and sensual small talk, cloaked in seemingly mundane words, Joan breathed out, "I didn't ask one. You did."

His eyebrows worked. His mouth twitched. He frowned. "I did?"

Joan grinned at his stiff *Gunfight at the OK Corral* stance. "You aren't getting any blood to your brain right now, are you?"

"No, I'm not, thanks to you and your legs. It's all in my pants." With that, he jerked toward the unmade bed and upended onto it the shopping bag's contents. From what Joan could see, he'd bought her everything she'd asked for. Even the sweater. Now she felt bad. She'd been teasing about all that stuff. *Oh, he's so sweet.*

Rummaging through the jumbled items, he snatched up his prize and turned to her, holding it up. A whole box of condoms. "For us," he said.

"Well, forget that thought. You aren't sweet."

"I might be—you don't know...yet." With that, Dan's expression again intensified, darkening with desire.

An answering bolt of heat arced through Joan, warming her body, her thoughts. This man wanted her. And he was every inch the healthy, red-blooded, sexually mature adult male that he appeared to be. And she wanted him. Now.

"Uncuff me." Was that whiskey voice hers?

Dan tossed the box onto the nightstand and strode to her with all the self-assurance of a prowling jungle cat. Standing in front of her, staring down at her, he wordlessly reached into his jeans' pocket. His muscles bunched under his knit shirt in an unconscious display of male grace and power. Joan all but slid out of the chair to the carpet.

He finally and mercifully came up with the key and freed her, stepping back to allow her room to stand. In a desire-fogged glide, she came to her feet. Dan immediately snagged her robe's ties and looped them around his hands, pulling her close. His gaze slid from her face to those exposed parts of her body now bared to his eyes.

She watched his face as he roved his gaze over her form. Then he met her eyes. "You're like a banquet. And I'm a starving man. You are so damned beautiful. I knew you would be."

Joan's breath came through her opened mouth. "Love me, Dan."

"Nothing would make me happier," he whispered as he freed his hands to slip them inside her robe. His fingers were long and strong, his skin warm, his touch questing. He encircled her waist, smoothing his hands around her ribs, settling them against her back. Abruptly, possessively, he pulled her to him. Joan gasped at the hunger evident in his eyes. Dan then claimed her mouth in the most soulful kiss she'd ever experienced.

She went up on tiptoe, her arms finding their own way

around his neck. He felt so good and hot and hard against her. Even with his gun under his shirt and wedged between their bodies. Dan's hands slid to her buttocks, cupped them, held her against him as his mouth took hers, demanding more and more from her. When he finally broke their kiss, he was having as much trouble breathing as she was.

"I've wanted to do this," he said huskily, his eyelids drooping sexily, "from the first second I opened the door to Interview Room 3."

Joan fisted her hands in his hair and smiled up at him. "Like I told you yesterday, I would've let you."

His eyes widened at her words. "Oh, son of a..." he murmured on an exhalation of warm breath. As if time was suddenly a factor, he smoothed the robe off her shoulders, letting it drop to the floor. His breath caught again. He scooped her up in his arms and carried her to the bed. Sitting her on it, he swiped all his purchases off the sheets and started undressing.

Arranging herself against the pillows at her back, Joan greedily watched. He breathed in as he tugged his shirt up to pull his gun free and set it on the nightstand. Then he undid his belt and popped open his pants' closure in two smooth motions. Not looking away from her, he finished tugging his knit shirt out of his jeans and, crossing his arms, grabbed its ends and lifted it off over his head.

Joan's fingers went to her mouth, stopping the hungry cry that tipped against her teeth. He was magnificent. Muscled, tanned, broad-shouldered, with a sprinkling of dark and crisply curling black hair adorning his chest, concentrating itself across his pecs and thinning to a line that slipped below his boxers' waistband. If he didn't hurry...! As if sensing her thoughts, Dan hurried. He turned and sat on the bed to work his boots and socks off. Then he stood, his back to her, and slid out of his jeans and boxers in one movement.

That's it. Joan darn near passed out. What a butt the man had. And the legs of a running-back. And then he turned to face her. Joan stared, heard the little sound she made, and held her hands up and out to him. Dan accepted that invitation. He knelt forward onto the mattress and stalked his way up the bed to her, right between her legs, focusing on her with such naked intent that the geometric planes of his face, its hollows and shadows alone, staggered her.

And then, Dan settled himself atop her, scooping her into his embrace, lifting her to him, his lips seeking her jaw, her neck, and down to her breasts, which he kissed with the same loving tenderness he had her mouth. Clutching at his arms, her nails digging into his skin, Joan gasped and cried out with need, "I can't wait, Dan. Now. Please. I need you."

Dan raised his head and met her gaze. "All right. This time." And then rolled off her to reach for the box of condoms. After a few moments of activity, he was back and exploring her body, his every touch claiming her. Joan suspected that in her entire life she'd never want any other man but this one to have his hands on her.

Dan now settled at her side, his leg hooked over hers, drawing hers apart. He kissed her mouth and slipped his hand down to the vee of her legs, stroking the pulsating warmth there until she arched against his hand and moaned into his mouth. Accepting that as his signal, he covered her, settling into the saddle of her hips and pressing against her, seeking entrance. Joan's body was ready for him, opened for him. He slipped inside her and stilled, sliding his hands under her shoulders to hold her to him.

She moaned. He all but growled and clung to her. Joan wrapped her legs around his hips and met his first and subsequent powerful thrusts with her own. This way they rocked and rocked together. She pulled his head down to her and kissed his mouth with all the fevered intensity centered in her womb. When their kiss broke, he arched himself upward, slanting more and more into her as she gripped the rock-hard, straining muscles of his arms.

And then it happened. Their very own rhythm brought them to the coiled pitch of their desire, until all else in the world dropped away, until all else was meaningless. Only this. Only this loving embrace. Joan rode the crest of her hungry wanting, gasping with each undulating spasm that clutched Dan inside her until a hoarse cry escaped him and he went rigid over her. He held himself there for breathless moments before collapsing atop her, drawing her to him and holding her.

Slick with loving wetness, her hair damp and tangled all around her, Joan stroked Dan's back and reveled in the sensations. The gentle pulsing of him still inside her. His weight shielding her from an unkind world. His embrace warming her, making her feel safe. She felt as if she and he floated on a cloud to a place where, as long as this man was there, the skies were blue forever.

After a quiet, content while, Dan roused, raising onto his elbows to brace himself above her. His face still dusky with desire, his mouth wet with her kiss, he grinned at her, devastating her with his sated sensuality. He shook his head slowly, saying, "It's like I've known you all my life. We just...*fit* together. Like we were made for each other and have already done this a million times."

Joan blinked and grinned at him, thrilled that there was none of the "afterward" awkwardness. Her arms went around his neck. "A million times, huh?"

"Well, until the condoms run out."

Joan stilled, raised her chin. "And then?"

"And then we'll buy more." He kissed the tip of her nose.

Joan chuckled and smacked at his arm. Dan shifted his weight, withdrew and rolled off her. "Think we can hit the one-million mark before this snow melts?" Then, lying flat out, looking like a model of male perfection painted by one of the Old Masters, he reached for the telephone on the nightstand, lifted the receiver off the hook and began pushing numbers.

Joan turned on her side. "What are you doing? The phone lines are dead."

Crossing his legs at the ankles, he glanced over at her as he put the receiver to his ear. "Are they?"

She waited. He didn't hang it up, but he did grin and wink at her. Coming to wary attention, Joan sat up. "Dan Hendricks, who are you calling? And why?"

He waved her to silence. "Shh. I'm calling the gift shop to see how many more boxes of condoms they have."

She laughed at this unexpected bit of fun from him and fell back against the pillows, watching him, reveling in the sight of his naked glory. "You are not."

He again flapped a hand at her to be quiet. "Shh. I got someone here. Hello? This is Dan Hendricks, up in room 412. I've got a pretty hot babe in my bed, and I was wondering how many—"

Joan screeched and made a dive for him.

WHICH WAS MORE DISTRACTING? Joan tried to decide. Dan's big and sprawling body pushed up next to her on the comfy couch, tucked into an alcove of the third-floor library? Or his heated murmurings as she read a much-thumbed romance novel she'd found on the shelves? Having reread the same page five times—aloud to him at his insistence—she sighed and firmly closed the paperback.

Chuckling and unrepentant, he pulled her to him, nuzzling her ear as he whispered, "Come on, read some more. I like that love scene."

"I know." Nearly panting from his touch, his kiss, the sound of his voice, the words on the page, Joan begged, "Stop it. I'm about to—" She bit back the heated words.

"Are you—right here? I think I like that. Am I... bothering you, Mrs. Thompson?"

"All the time." Joan hit at him, trying her best not to grin. "I missed lunch because of you. And already it's nearly three o'clock."

"Can't you just be hungry for me?" he crooned in her ear, his voice no more than a feathery whisper. "You look mighty nice in that new sweater, ma'am. And even nicer out of it. Speaking of that, how many more condoms do we have left? Do I need to make a trip to the gift shop? Although that nice lady working there thinks I'm interested in her, as many times as I've stopped by."

Joan elbowed his ribs. "Will you stop that? You have been in there one time. And you didn't call anybody, you big fake. There wasn't even a dial tone." She moved his questing hand away from her...thigh, and warned, "Stop it. I can only take so much. And you're embarrassing me. You do know we're not alone, don't you?"

"Aren't we?" His husky voice made the words an endearment, but he pulled away to lean forward until he could see the room at large. "Oooh, baby," he crooned as he sat back, staring at her. "Houston, we have a problem."

Dread for what she'd see swamped Joan. "Oh, no," she groaned, following his gaze. Yep. There they were. The whites of the old folks' eyes as they stared in wary attentiveness. Well, she'd certainly done her work here, hadn't she? She laid her book down, telegraphing a reassuring smile and a shake of her head to signal that Dan wasn't having an episode.

"Quit that." Dan yanked her back to him.

Seeing the amused twinkling in his eyes that belied his show of…distemper, Joan wrinkled her nose at him. "Well, your behavior is shocking them, Sheriff. Now behave—you're being bad."

He chuckled. "I told you—it's part of my charm." He smoothed her hair back so he could rub his knuckle up and down her neck. "Besides, I thought you liked it when I was bad. That was you, wasn't it, upstairs, moaning under me all morning? And part of the afternoon?"

A certain swollen, tender part of Joan's anatomy jumped to pulsating life. She elbowed her tormentor's ribs. "Behave. I'm warning you."

"You are? Behave or what?" Dan pulled back, showering her with a dazzling grin.

Joan crossed her arms as she leaned over to him. "Do you want me to tell them you're…" She whispered a really decadent something in his ear.

Dan jerked back, raising his hands as if he'd been placed under arrest. "Point taken, ma'am. Backing off and behaving."

A sudden commotion in the cozy room had Joan looking around. Two skittish ladies lurched to their feet, apparently ready to flee. Joan waved a hand to reassure them. "It's okay. He was just…um, repeating his key phrase that stops unwanted behaviors." Well, it sounded good to her. "Now, please stay, Mrs. Compton, Mrs. Edwards. You too, Mr. Garrison."

The two plump, stiffly coiffed matrons exchanged a look, apparently drew courage from each other and sat, raising their books high to hide their faces. Mr. Garrison, however, eyed her and Dan in a speculative way. *Great. Here goes.*

Sure enough, "Mr. Thompson, I'm not much for pryin', but what is it you do for a livin'?" the New Englander pried.

9
_____

WHEN DAN DIDN'T RESPOND, Joan glanced over at him and rolled her eyes. "Give me that," she ordered, pulling the romance novel from his hands. His eyebrows lowered like a Neanderthal's. Joan gripped his chin and turned his head until he faced her. "Pay attention. Mr. Garrison is talking to you. He wants to know what you do for a living."

Despite her grip on him, Dan effortlessly turned his head and shot Mr. Garrison a look before whispering to her, "So what *do* I do?"

"I never said. Use your imagination." Joan finally turned him loose and sat back, crossing her legs.

"Oh, hell," Dan muttered as Mr. Garrison pulled a chair up in front of them and sat with his knees spread, his hands braced atop them. Dan nodded his head, saying "Howdy" by way of greeting the white-haired, smiling little man.

"Howdy yourself, big fella," Mr. Garrison returned. "Been thinkin' about that gun you tote. And them handcuffs. Some of us were talking over our bridge game last evenin' about what it might be that you do to put bread on your table. Found we couldn't even begin to guess, given your...special personality."

Dan shot Joan a this-is-all-your-fault look and again focused on the inquisitive older fellow. Adopting a sober expression, Dan said, "It's a secret." Joan surreptitiously pinched his arm. He didn't even flinch.

"A secret, is it?" Mr. Garrison echoed, leaning forward, his brown eyes alight. "How secret?"

Dan leaned forward until his forehead almost touched Mr. Garrison's. "So secret," he said, "that if I told you, I'd have to kill you. And in a way that would hurt. You still want to know?"

Apparently all pluck and daring, and all yellow-velour jogging suit, Mr. Garrison said, "Ah-yep, so go ahead and tell me."

"Yeah," Joan encouraged. "Go ahead. Tell him, dear."

Dan swiveled to give her the evil eye. She grinned back at him. His hazel eyes lit with humor, but he produced a properly serious scowl for his geriatric Grand Inquisitor. "All right. But you have to swear you won't tell a living soul. Not even your lovely missus."

Mr. Garrison casually flicked his right hand up to the oath-taking position and then resettled it atop his knee. "So sworn."

Dan nodded, opened his mouth to speak. Joan leaned forward. *This* she had to hear. The sound of shifting weight, of fabric rubbing against fabric, coming from the matching Queen Anne chairs told her Mrs. Compton and Mrs. Edwards were no longer reading, either. Dan quirked an amused but devilish expression Joan's way that had her suddenly fearing this monster she'd created.

Sure enough, he told Mr. Garrison, "I'm a crash-test aviator for a high-level governmental organization that specializes in defensive aerobatic maneuvers to deflect unfriendlies with extreme prejudice in adverse meteorological and warfare combat conditions under strictest lock-down and quadrilateral efforts by the joint commands and forces with the biennial treaty agreements co-signed by us and our most-favored-nation status allies in the western hemisphere.'' He paused, drew a breath, and added, ''Including Antarctica.''

Joan's muscles locked. Her eyes bugged. Dead silence to echo hers came from the Queen Anne chairs. However, Mr. Garrison nodded, never lost a beat. ''One of those, eh? I've heard of 'em.''

''Have you now?'' Dan drawled. Joan awarded him points for keeping a straight face.

''Ah-yep. Read a story back home in the papers about your organization. I said to the wife it'd be kind of hard to fit all that on a name tag.'' Mr. Garrison waited, looked from one to the other of them. Then he scratched his white hair, thoroughly mussing it. ''Well, the wife thought it was funny.'' Now he pointed at Dan. ''Explain them handcuffs. The paper never said you types carried handcuffs, young fella.''

Biting the inside of her cheek to keep from laughing aloud at this game of one-upmanship, Joan waited. Dan favored her with another thanks-a-lot look. She smiled, loving this discomfiture of his. But he didn't. Smile, that is. Instead, he shook his head and refocused on the old gentleman, finally confessing, ''In my spare time, I'm a cop.''

Mr. Garrison sat back and crossed his arms over his chest. ''Thought as much. Told Ethel—that's the missus—you had the look of the law about you.''

Now for *that*, Joan had a comeback. She jerked her thumb toward Dan, capturing for herself the men's gazes. But a sudden movement in the hallway captured her attention. Instantaneous and heart-thumping fright imprisoned her breath in her lungs. She clutched Dan's arm. He covered her hand with his own. ''What's wrong?''

With a taut jerk of her head, she now stared at him, whispering, ''It's…him. I think.''

A split second's frown of confusion shadowed Dan's features before he evidently caught her meaning and directed his steely gaze to the hallway. She followed suit and, having to look past Mr. Garrison to the hallway behind him, Joan saw their companion had taken notice of their brief, whispered exchange. The sharp old man's eyes narrowed briefly before he wrenched around in his chair to see what concerned her and Dan.

But Mr. Garrison, Dan, the library—indeed, the world—blurred to the outer reaches of Joan's awareness as the stranger out in the hallway claimed the clear-lensed center of her attention. As if on cue, the man slowed his steps, turned his head, zeroed in on her. Joan expected a rush of fear to course through her. But how could it? The man staring at her had a face made for comedy clubs. Thick eyeglasses. Black, bushy eyebrows, and mustache to match. Like three caterpillars had taken up residence on his face. Short, thick, and squat of body, in dark clothes. Yeah, all that. Maybe that's what caught her attention. But so momentarily frightened had she been that she still couldn't look away from him.

Until Dan's voice broke the spell. He spoke to her in soft and soothing tones. "Is that him?"

Before Joan could recover her balance, Mr. Garrison faced them again, his gaze darting from her face to Dan's. "Interestin' fella, that one. Reminds me of Groucho Marx. Got here the same day we did, but a few hours later. That was the day before you skied up. Friendly sort. A real talker, but an eye for the ladies. Have a care for your bride there, Mr. Thompson."

Joan wrenched her gaze to the older man. But Dan spoke for her. "A ladies' man, huh? Thanks for the insight. I'll do that."

Mr. Garrison scratched his head. His hair spiked straight up where he rubbed. "Be a good idea. I've told Ethel—

that's the missus—ta keep away from him. She's quite a looker, you know...like your missus here. And what he does for a livin' don't help matters none."

Joan exchanged a look with Dan, and asked what Mr. Garrison so obviously wanted one of them to. "And what does he do for a living?"

"A perfume salesman," the older man blurted. "Them cheap kinds, too. The designer-label rip-offs. Most likely illegal, if you ask me. Why, the man smells like a cheap whor—um, to high heavens. Totes them samples everywhere he goes, too, giving 'em to all the women. I don't mind telling you, some of us men are thinkin' of havin' a talk with him, if you get my drift." Now he focused on Dan. "Be interested to know your take on this, young fella."

"As a policeman? Or a husband?"

The word came out of his mouth so naturally that Joan could only stare at Dan's profile. He glanced in her direction, winked at her, and then refocused on Mr. Garrison, leaving Joan's heart to beat a tattoo against her ribs.

"Both, I suppose," Mr. Garrison was saying.

"Well," Dan began, "as a policeman, I'd say you have every right to talk to the man—if by 'talk' you mean 'talk,' and that's all. But speaking as a husband, I suggest we kick his butt."

Joan gasped in surprise. But Mr. Garrison chuckled. "I like you, young fella. We think alike when it comes to protecting our womenfolk."

Protecting our womenfolk? Excuse me? Is this the 1990s...or the 1890s? The thought was there, but she didn't get too worked up over the older man's attitude, knowing he was from a previous generation. But then...

"Now if only we could find someone to protect us from our womenfolk, right, Mr. Garrison?" Dan quipped.

So much for male bonding. ''All right, you two, that's enough,'' Joan cut in, garnering for herself two sets of wide-eyed and innocent gazes. She stood up. ''Don't make me go for reinforcements—and I mean in the kitchen to get the other women to help me raise your consciousness. Maybe with a rolling pin.''

IN THE HALLWAY, just lumbering past the library, Bruno hurried his steps and twitched his nose, trying his best to resettle the fake eyeglasses and not to scratch the itchy mustache glued under his nose. All he needed to do was accidentally pull the furry thing off his face. Or worse, knock it sideways and not know it. That would give him away in a second. And the boss wasn't none too pleased with him, as it was. So if he gave himself away, if he blew this one last chance to kill the girl who'd seen him kill Tony, the boss would send someone to nail him.

All this thinking. It made his head hurt—even worse than his arm had when he got his tattoo. Or maybe it was all the perfume samples he had to tote around as part of his disguise. Why hadn't he picked a fake job in some field he wasn't allergic to? But he'd had to think quick—never an easy thing for him, as the boss said—when the Taos cops started getting wise to his being there and asking around about the girl. That's when he'd given himself a fake job, in case anyone asked him what he did for a living, and come up here to lay low. Who'd have thought she'd end up here, too? Bruno grinned, still not believing his good luck. The boss would be happy, too, that he could finish the job.

Still, it was a shame to have to kill her. She was a good-looking babe, not like all those other old ladies here that he had to kiss up to. Bruno sighed. Just part of the job, pretending to like some folks, having to kill other ones, nice ones you might've liked to date otherwise. But that was out, the dating part. She was with that big deputy. Bruno recognized him from when he was keeping an eye out for the cops in Taos. So that fake story of theirs, about being honeymooners, hadn't fooled him. The cop brought her up here to hide her from him, Bruno Taglia. He snorted. And the boss said he was dumb. The cop had brought her to him on a silver platter. Well, skis, he supposed.

But now the lawman posed a problem. The boss wouldn't like it none if he had to take out a cop. Too much heat. But he might not be able to help it, if he was to get to the girl. And he'd have to do it soon, too. He'd seen the look she just gave him, heard her gasp. She suspected him. Bruno shoved open the heavy fire door that led to the stairway and shuffled down the steps. Tonight, then. It had to be tonight. At the social get-together the old ladies were planning. Now to see how to disable that emergency power generator out back.

"HEY, sit down, you, you're not going anywhere," Dan assured Joan, accompanying his words with a chuckle. "We've got all the reinforcements we need in here." He pointed to Mrs. Edwards and Mrs. Compton.

Joan sat, but that didn't mean she wasn't annoyed as heck with both men. Womenfolk, indeed. It also didn't mean that she was over her fright from seeing that Groucho guy who was just too much like the hit man for her comfort. But right then, another figure appeared in the library's archway to capture her attention. Praise be, this time it was only a young male lodge employee, who spotted them and leaned into the room, addressing Dan. "Mr. Jacobs sent me to find you. He said to tell you he's in his office…that it would mean something to you?"

Joan looked over at Dan to see him nodding. And looking grim. "Yeah, it does. Thanks. Tell him we'll be right there."

When the dark-haired kid nodded and left, Joan searched Dan's face, but he offered nothing, merely gripped her arm and pulled her to her feet along with him. Mr. Garrison also stood, and Dan nodded to him. "If you'll excuse us, the missus and I have to, uh, go do something in the office."

Mr. Garrison waved them away. "I heard. Don't stay on my account. I have to see to a nap, myself." He started to turn away, but added, "See you tonight at the sing-along?"

"What sing-along?" Joan asked. Dan stilled next to her. Suspiciously so.

Mr. Garrison raised a bushy eyebrow at Dan and then addressed Joan. "The one in the lobby. Around that old piano. The ladies organized it, told everyone at breakfast, including your mister here. So join us. Can't stay up in your room all the time, honeymooners or not. There'll be cider and cookies. Ought to be fun."

"That's what I thought," came Dan's deadpanned sentiment as he tugged on Joan's arm, obviously wanting to be gone.

Joan resisted, accusing him with a slanted look before she turned to Mr. Garrison. "It does sound like fun. And thank you for telling *me* about it, since *no one* else did." Dan muttered something under his breath that Joan didn't catch but did ignore in favor of telling Mr. Garrison, "We'd love to come. What time?"

"After supper. Sevenish. See you then." With that, Mr. Garrison turned, called out a goodbye to Mrs. Compton and Mrs. Edwards and shuffled off across the room, making his way toward the hallway. An absently executed wave with a knobby-knuckled hand punctuated his exit.

Joan glanced Dan's way, saw him watching Mr. Garrison

take his leave. Then he surprised her by calling out, "Mr. Garrison?"

The older man stopped and turned around, his eyebrows raised in anticipation of a question, which Dan asked. "I was just wondering, sir, what do *you* do to put bread on your table?"

Mr. Garrison's brown-eyed gaze sparked, as much as saying he'd hoped he'd be asked this. His sly grin nailed Joan and Dan in place like mounted trophies on a hunting-lodge wall. But what he said was, "I'm retired, young fella. My pension puts bread on my table." With that and a wink, the old man turned around and walked slowly toward the exit. "See you at supper," he said in parting as he rounded the corner to his left and disappeared from view.

Joan steadfastly stared at the spot just vacated by the harmless older man. Then she turned to Dan. "Do you get the feeling there's more to him than he's telling?"

His eyes alight with mischief, Dan's mock-accusing stare fell on her. "Why not? There's certainly more to us, *Barbie,* than we're letting on. What a story you stuck us with." Then his gaze roved over her, heating her, and by the looks of his heightened color, heated him, too. "But I guess I shouldn't complain. Being newlyweds has its moments. Like now." He grabbed her arms, pulled her tight against his chest and growled low in his throat as he bent his head to her neck, pretending to take a bite out of her.

Joan shrieked, but not nearly as loudly as Mrs. Compton and Mrs. Edwards. Their flurry of prayerful activity, over by the Queen Anne chairs, pulled the happy couple apart, had them jerking around in surprise to see two blurs of motion. Wide-eyed with fear, staring at Joan and Dan, the grandmotherly types sidled along the wall and then all but galloped out of the library and down the hallway.

A long silence ensued. Joan finally blinked, exhaling as she turned away from the again-deserted doorway to look at Dan. "I forgot all about them. What must they think?"

He grinned at her. "That we're newlyweds?"

"Will you please tell me how we—in the space of ten minutes—went from me kissing your neck in the library to you griping at me about not telling you about the sing-along?" While he asked, Dan rapped a knuckle against the lodge office's closed door and then called out, "It's me, Mark."

Then he resumed his monologue with Joan, who apparently was not talking to him, judging by her averted gaze and pointed silence. "Will you look at me, please?" She wouldn't. Dan made a noise of disgust and added, "Do you know what this means, why we're standing here? The phone lines must be working. Which means I can call the station and start getting you cleared."

Just as she opened her mouth and gathered a breath, obviously preparing to tell him her thoughts, Mark opened the door. And surprised Dan by blocking their entry while he seriously scrutinized them—as if this were a top-secret facility and he had to verify their identities.

"It's really us, Mark," Dan sniped. "And I don't think we were followed, so let us in. Or is there a secret code word I'm supposed to know?"

Mark's face colored. Joan chose that moment to speak up. But she spoke to Mark. "Has he always been bossy like this?"

"Since I've known him. His way or the highway." With that, he motioned them inside.

Dan wasn't taking this lying down. "You're still ticked because I was chosen football captain in the ninth grade."

"And every year after that," Mark added with a grin.

He leaned over toward Joan, mock whispering, "It's always the quarterback who gets to be captain."

Joan whispered right back, "And the girls. I hear they get the girls, too."

"That's enough," Dan cut in. He punctuated his words by dragging his ponytailed prisoner into the room with him, closing the door behind them and pointing her to a chair pushed against the room's back wall. "Have a seat and stay there. Can you do that, or do I need to cuff you?"

As he watched, Joan marched to the vinyl-upholstered chair and flopped down heavily on it. She then directed a Grim Reaper smile at Dan, saying, "I think I'm capable of sitting here, Sheriff. But since you get your jollies by hand-cuffing me, then—"

"Just sit there." Dan arrowed a glance at Mark, whose face was as red as he figured his own was. "She says things like that all the time, just to shock people."

Mark nodded. "Sounds to me like she knows you, buddy."

Dan put his hands to his waist. "Whose side are you on?"

A big grin split Mark's face as he pointed past Dan to Joan, who sat up straighter in her chair. "Hers."

Dan caught himself before an answering chuckle escaped him. Instead, he shook his head, quirked his mouth into a grimace. "Damned defensive linesmen. Never were too smart." Then he got down to business. "All right, let's see what I can do about making everything okay—"

"Ha! Don't believe him." This from Joan. Dan pivoted to her, gave her a look, but it did no damned good. "The last time he said that to me, his plane crashed and we nearly got eaten by bears."

"Will you just sit there and accept that staying with me, instead of visiting with the ladies in the kitchen, is for your own good, Joan? You're just safer here with me. Where I can keep an eye on you.''

''I'm safer? Or are you?''

''All right, I am.''

She crossed her arms under her little-children-of-the-world sweater-covered bosom. ''Well, you won't be when Mrs. Compton and Mrs. Edwards tell everyone that you growled and bit me on my neck right in front of them. I'm telling you, you better let me go talk to them—before they combine forces and bash you in the head.''

Dan ignored the shocked gasp from Mark, and the burning heat on his own cheeks, to tell Joan, ''Is that why you're mad? Because I won't let you go tell them some cockeyed story about me being a werewolf—which is exactly what you'd do, isn't it?''

''I might.'' With that, she snatched a touristy-type magazine from the round wood-block table next to her and began flipping pages.

Effectively dismissed, Dan exhaled and turned back to Mark, who said, ''Man, you are in over your head. It's about time.''

''Shut up, Mark,'' Dan griped. He knew it. So he didn't need anyone else telling him. In silence, he watched Mark make his way behind the desk. His big blond pal put the telephone receiver to his ear and punched the different incoming lines, all the while listening. Dan sat on one of the chairs that faced the desk and begged, ''Tell me it's still working.''

Mark nodded. ''Yep. Up and running. For now, anyway, given all the rain and flooding going on down in the valley. I heard about it on my transistor radio, right before the batteries went dead.''

Dan spared a fatalistic chuckle for that. ''Man, that's par

for the course.'' Then he took the receiver when Mark held it out to him, adding, ''What we need are cell phones.''

''But first we'd have to have cell sites, right? I'll go get the guest register, so you can give the names to Cal. Ask him if they're building an ark yet. If so, tell him the only things we have two of up here are men and women.''

Dan couldn't resist. ''But only one woman capable of breeding in the new post-flood world.''

''Ha, ha, Hendricks,'' she retorted to his back. He tensed, fully expecting to get clobbered at any second. Sure enough, the clobber came, but with words muttered not quite under her breath. ''As if you'd have a chance.''

Dan's gaze locked with Mark's, whose eyebrows shot up. He pointed and tripped his way to the closed door, mumbling, ''I'll just get that register...with the names... and check on supper...while th—'' He made it to the door, jerked it open and fled through it, closing it sharply behind him.

Alone now with his shy little ''bride,'' Dan pivoted, bracing an arm across the chair's back. She looked up at him, green eyes edged with defiance, cherry mouth puckered with the same emotion. All spit and fire to cover her fear, her helplessness...her needing him. Dan's heart melted, bringing a smile to his face. ''You okay?''

Tears sprang to her eyes, but she said, ''As I'll ever be.''

''You know, you're brave as hell. You've been through a lot and yet you don't give up. You keep pushing. I like that about you.'' Dan watched her reaction, saw her blink, swallow and raise her chin. He winked, too full of his own sudden emotion to do anything but turn his back to her and dial the number to the department.

As it rang, he forced his thoughts to what he needed to say. Then Cal answered. Dan surprised himself with how excited he felt, like a kid on his birthday. So much had happened, so much still needed to happen. "Cal, it's me, Dan. Yeah, we made it to the lodge. Hear it's raining cats and dogs— What? Old Shep's home? Are you kidding?"

He pivoted, telling Joan, "That's my grandfather's dog. He's as bad as the old man." Then Dan went silent. Her eyes were still suspiciously shiny. Had no one ever told her she was brave? Poor kid. Taking a deep breath around the tightness in his chest, Dan faced forward again and listened. "He brought what—that collie with him? Puppies? That's what we need. Ad? What ad? Tell me you're lying." Again he turned to Joan. "Grandpa took an ad out in the paper inviting all of Taos to his wedding on Halloween."

"Oh, lovely." She grinned. "Whatever shall we wear?"

She sobered at the same moment Dan did. His gaze locked with hers. The implication—that she might be in his life then—spread a warmth to his heart, and a frown to his face. Was that where they were headed? To a life together?

"Dan," Joan urged, "remember Pam and Bob Jackson. And my friends."

"Yeah." He turned away from her, put the receiver to his ear. "Cal, do me a favor, man. I need you to call some folks in Houston and tell them Joan's okay." He gave him the names and then added, "So, despite falling out of airplanes and getting stuck in a tree, I've also found time to solve the LoBianco murder." He jerked the receiver away from his ear, waited a second, and then put it back. "Settle down, man. Okay, I'll wait. Go get them. Yeah, put me on the speakerphone."

Behind him, the office door opened. Dan turned, saw Mark coming in with the guest register, which he held out to him. As he took it, Dan said, "Thanks, man. I owe you, big time."

Mark waved that away, and jerked a thumb over his

shoulder. "I've got a situation in the kitchen—too many cooks. I'm just going to slip out."

Dan nodded, heard Sheriff Halverson's booming greeting in his ear. "I'm fine, sir. Thanks. Yes, that's right, I know what happened and who did it. Just not what he looks like, or what his name is. Or why. Yes sir, *he*. No, not her. I know, confusing."

To prove it, Sheriff Halverson went ballistic. All Dan could do was listen and gesture and shake his head and try to cut in. "Yes, sir, I know what's at stake— The killer's probably that same— No, it's not— Yes, we're safe here. I'll be careful, yes. I appreciate that. I know. What? No, it wasn't Miss O'Leary. Yes, sir, I'm sure." Having won the floor with that, Dan launched into how he knew Joan wasn't guilty.

Several minutes later, his luck and the phone line still holding, Dan got to the names in the guest register, telling Ben Halverson he'd like them to double-check everyone here, just to be sure Joan was safe. No sense taking chances. Then he waited, hearing through the lines a flurry of activity. He could just see the scene now—everyone getting pen and paper, Cal on the computer and ready to input, the phone call going to the D.A. But what he liked best was the note of pride in Ben Halverson's voice and how he called him son. "Yes, sir. You ready? Okay, here's the first name I need you to— Hello? Hello?"

This is not happening. Dan sat stock-still, staring straight ahead at a framed restaurant association certificate hanging on the wall. The phone line was dead. He whirled to tell Joan. Her chair was empty. His gut twisted. He slammed down the receiver in its cradle and jumped up, turning to the office door…which was ajar.

A howling string of epithets accompanied his running steps out of the ground-floor office and across the lobby's flagstones. He took the split-log stairs two at a time, sprinting to the second-floor kitchen—empty. Hadn't Mark said something about too many cooks? Where was everyone? More alarmed by the second, Dan jetted back to the stairs, took them in a headlong flight and didn't slow down until he jerked to a stop in front of his room.

Breathing hard, crazy with worry, he fumbled in his jeans' pocket for the room key. Finally, his fingers and the denim cooperated, allowing him to extract it. In the next second, he held his Beretta in his other hand. Only then did he put the key to the lock—and freeze. The door was already open. Alarm shot through him.

He retreated from the doorway, took a couple of calming breaths, forced himself to think. *Just follow police procedure.* He did, plastering his back to the hallway wall and listening. He heard things being bumped and knocked about, whispering, the closet sliding open, drawers being pulled out. Dan's jaw set with rage. His eyes narrowed. That was not Joan. She'd have no reason to rummage through their room like that. She knew where everything was.

Then that meant, just as he'd feared, she wasn't safe here. But whoever this was, they'd be sorry. Especially if they'd so much as harmed a hair on her head. Deadly grim, and ready as he'd ever be, Dan jerked away from the wall, twisted to face the room, kicked the door open and burst inside, leading with his gun and yelling, ''Police! I'm with the police and I'm armed. Freeze! Put your hands up or I'll shoot!''

10

THAT EVENING'S GATHERING around the lobby's ill-tuned piano—despite the sugar cookies and the cider, the out-of-tune singing and the cloyingly cheerful camaraderie—could do nothing to lift Dan's dark cloud of doom and gloom. And lingering embarrassment. Thus, he was happy that the milling, buzzing, visiting beehive of a crowd, made up of virtually everyone else staying at the lodge, was ignoring him over here in his little corner of the room on the big couch all by himself.

To prove that he didn't care, he slouched down on the thick cushions, crossed his arms over his chest and evil-eyed the throng. He didn't want to sing, anyway. And he sure as heck didn't want cookies and cider, not even if they were offered to him. Least of all did he want any part of the sharing of personal tales, all that snowed-in bonding. Furthermore, he really didn't like any of these people. And he wanted to go home. To Grandpa and Old Shep. The guys.

Speaking of guys, what about this middle-aged Romeo with the Groucho Marx eyeglasses, eyebrows and matching mustache? Was he for real? His appearance aside, what bugged Dan more was the way he bird-dogged Joan's every step. If Groucho didn't knock it off, Dan silently threatened, he'd have to pull his gun and shoot the yutz from here. Drastic? Yeah. But any other course of action involved getting up off the couch. Which might mean he'd have to trade pleasantries—before and after the shooting. He focused inward, checked his mood. No. Definitely precluded making nice.

Since when did you start having moods, Hendricks? Oh, about two days ago, he answered himself, playing his life in reverse from right now on the couch to all the way back to Interview Room 3, and then forward again to now. It suddenly occurred to him that he had no idea what he used to do with his time, pre-Joan. *Great. She's taken over. Hogtied and domesticated, that's me.*

A sudden and cryptic vision of himself in another six months—standing in a mall, lost, holding a bunch of packages *and* Joan's purse while she shopped, and himself wearing a Have You Seen My Wife? T-shirt—made mingling, in the interest of police work, very attractive. Very macho. As if he really had a choice, given that the phone lines had never come back on. Which meant the guests remained who they said they were, that he had to accept them at face value. Or he could use the human approach—talk to folks, see what he could glean from their words and attitudes.

Thinking along those lines, Dan glanced around the crowded room at the cheerfully milling people across the way and realized that the piano's ivories were no longer being tortured. No reprieve, then. Time to chat up the strandees. Up and at 'em, Dan. His antisocial grimace deepened as he started to pull himself off the couch. But he wasn't quick enough. He never even had a chance to get out of the way before Joan startled him with her apparition-like appearance. Just *poof*—she was there and merrily plopping down beside him on the couch, a mug of hot sloshing cider in one hand, a fistful of cookies in the other. "Howdy, stranger," she greeted him.

"Howdy, yourself." Dan grabbed her arm, extending it

and her dripping mug out over the flagstone flooring. "Let's not add third-degree burns to our excellent adventure, shall we?"

"Especially not to any sensitive areas, huh?"

"Especially." He mugged a grimace, but couldn't hold on to it, not in the face of her big grin. All right, so he couldn't stay mad at her. Hiding the sappy giddiness that her nearness caused him, Dan let go of her arm to brush her bangs out of her eyes. "What became of the screech-along?"

"Refreshment break," she cheerfully supplied, sticking a fistful of cookies under his nose. "Want one?"

He pulled back, brushing at her hand. "No, thanks. Aren't you afraid your new friends will be mad at you if they see you over here talking to me?"

"I would be, if I was in the seventh grade." Then, sounding as cheerful as a spring robin, she asked, "So, how long *are* you going to sit here behaving like a six-year-old who didn't get what he wanted from Santa?"

"Is that how it looks?" He glared at her jokingly. "What're you laughing at? Where's your boyfriend?"

Grinning, Joan eyed him and scooted back, settling herself right up against him. She crossed her legs on the cushions and took a particularly loud slurp of cider. "You mean Scott?"

"Aw, man." Dan chuckled. "That's low." His knees spread, his hands folded together atop his abdomen, he rolled his head until he could look into her teasing green eyes. "Not Scott. I'm talking about your current boyfriend."

"Oh. Groucho? I gave him the slip at the cider bowl. What a persistent little twerp." She leaned forward to set down her mug and the cookies. Then she swung back to him, leaning into his chest to rub noses with him, give him a quick kiss and whisper, "Kinda reminds me of you."

With her body pressed against his, Dan felt a quickening in his hinterland, but feigned being unaffected as he loosely held her to him. "We're talking about the persistent part, I hope. And it's lucky for you I am. Otherwise, I wouldn't know the truth. And if I hadn't held you hostage out in that blizzard, I'd never know how you feel about me. Or worse yet, just how you feel."

"There you go, being bad again." Joan chuckled as she pulled away and sank back into the cushions. "I guess you know I had my hands full convincing all these nice people that my life was not in any danger from you. Just as I feared, they were ready to mob you and lock you in a utility closet until the snowplows come through."

Veeing his eyebrows down over his nose, Dan sat up to pluck a sugar cookie off the table. Taking a bite, wiping crumbs off his freshly laundered denims, he talked with his mouth full. "Speaking of this afternoon, see if I have events straight. While I'm in Mark's office on the phone—busting my hump to clear your name—you slip away to attend a meeting of the Ken Thompson hate club, right?"

Joan chuckled and mouthed, "Uh-huh."

"Then I turn around, and you're gone. I'm looking all over for you, I'm frantic, I can't find anybody. So I take the stairs like an Olympic sprinter and hightail it to our room, praying you're not hurt or worse, when—picture this—I draw my gun and *burst* into our room, yelling I'm the cops, put your hands up. Only to scare the hell out of three blue-haired little old ladies going through our stuff."

Joan clamped a hand over her mouth, but her laughter-filled eyes gave her away. She made sounds like she was choking.

"It's not funny," Dan warned, fighting a grin himself.

"So there we are, they're yelling, I'm trying to calm them down, they're trying to get by me or kill me—I still don't know which. Then I realize I still have my gun drawn, which isn't helping, so I holster it, ask them what's going on. Big mistake. They trade looks and then start—now, here's the good part—undressing me and shouting how they need to do a load of laundry. *Need to,* mind you. Like the fate of the free world hinges on them rinsing out my boxers.''

Joan eyed him and then collapsed on herself, holding her sides and giggling uncontrollably. Chuckling now, Dan leaned over her and persisted with his version of events. "Obviously I chose not to roam the halls wearing your undies and the shower curtain. So tell me, how *did* those ladies get elected by the club to keep me in the room while you chaired your meeting?''

Joan flopped over on her back, a sensual picture with her auburn hair fanned out around her, and grinned at him. "They got the short straws. See, I knew you'd come looking for me, so we sent the three cutest ones to take you on. They were supposed to cry and make you feel bad and get you to cooperate with them. Worked, didn't it?''

Dan forced a pained expression onto his features. "Oh, yeah, it worked. They'd didn't leave me a stitch. I'm yelling where are you, they're yelling she's fine—she's with the men, she's with the men. I didn't find that fine at all. Then I get shoved into the bathroom. So there I am—stripping in fast-forward time, throwing my unmentionables out the door, trying to strip before they start that crying again. Or worse, barge in to finish the job.''

Joan zipped upright, as if she'd been pulled forward, and leered at him. "Ooh, you should've let them. They might've liked that.''

Dan sobered, painfully so, as he wagged his remaining

bit of cookie in her face. "Let's not sear that image into my brain. It would render me incapable of...performing. I'd have to become a monk. And you—you ought to be ashamed. These are little children's grandmas we're talking about." With that and a glare, he poked his cookie into his mouth and seriously chewed it.

But Joan the Bad met his gaze evenly. "So, tell me, just how do you think they got to be little childrens' grandmas, huh?" She batted her long eyelashes at him, managing to convey both innocence and wantonness.

Dan grimaced. "Don't even look at me like that. Or this afternoon in the library will be nothing to what these old folks will see right here." Joan's eyes widened and she wiped the wanton look off her face. Seeing that, Dan called a halt to the fun. "All right, O'Leary, move it. I need to go mingle and see what I can learn. See who in our little circle here is really who he says he is."

"Unlike us...right, Ken?" With that, she moved over—with a little more shoving help from him. And then leaned right back into him, whispering, "If you'll give me a kiss and promise to be in a better mood by bedtime, I'll tell you a story about a naughty female prisoner who seduced her sheriff—"

"Mercy." Dan did his best to ignore the tightening bulge in his jeans and shoved to his feet, leaning over her. "I'll wait for the movie to come out."

"Will you?" She gripped his shoulders and pulled him down to her.

Dan smacked a kiss on her sugarcoated, puckered mouth. Then, faking distaste, he ran his tongue over his lips. "Yuck. Cider." And cut off any response on her part with another kiss, this one deeper, more soulful. When he straightened up this time, she flopped limply, comically, onto the cushions.

"Another satisfied customer," Dan quipped as he, the very image of the strutting male, hitched at his denims and glanced around the crowded room. "So, who do you think I should drill first?"

A sustained silence from the couch had him pivoting to see her eyebrow-raised expression. He thought about what he'd said and amended, "Drill—in the sense of questioning closely."

"Well, now I have to change my answer." She sat up and surveyed the milling throng. "Let's see…okay, start with Groucho. The last I saw him, he was at the refreshment table Bogartin' all the cookies."

"You mean the few you left behind?"

She poked out her tongue at him and warned, "Now, look here, Sheriff—"

But he couldn't. Because that was the last he saw of her. At least, clearly. Because the electricity blinked off. No warning. No drama.

One second, all was light and happiness. The next, warm air no longer whooshed from vents, and all was deep blackness. Gasps of shock greeted this event. Instantly alert, Dan drew his gun and put a hand out to signal Joan to stay put. In that same instant, the lodge's automatic front door, around the corner and thus hidden from view, slinked open.

Dan, along with everyone else, turned in that direction. He tightened his grip on his gun but stayed where he was, fearing that this could be a diversion to get him away from Joan. A blast of cold air rushed into the room, and then the doors closed with the slow hiss of pneumatic smoothness.

The silence thickened like a fog as they all waited to see who would round the corner. But no one did. Folks shifted, tension mounted. The unspoken conclusion was…someone had just left the building. And it wasn't Elvis Presley, in all likelihood.

In the next whispering seconds, eyes adjusted to light cast by the leaping flames in the fireplace. Bursts of red and yellow lit the cathedral-ceilinged room and threw distorted shadows along the walls, giving the overall scene a hellish quality. Fearful questions bounced around the lobby, mingling with pleas for calm, calls of nothing to worry about, we'll just check the breaker fuses, this happens all the time.

Yeah, right, was Dan's reasoned response. He scanned the room for possible trouble headed his way, saw none, and then glanced down at Joan, telling her, "Stay right there. Don't move."

"Don't worry," came her immediate, whispered response. "Why do I think this power outage has nothing to do with the weather?"

"Probably for the same reason I don't." Then to the room at large, he called out, "Nobody move. Just stay calm, and don't anybody try to leave this lobby. Mark? Where are you?"

"Right here, buddy," he answered from somewhere across the room and over the worried murmurs of *It's him! That crazy young man from South Bend? The one married to that poor girl? Oh, dear, he has a gun. Do you suppose he did something to the electricity? We're all going to die.*

Dan made a face, hoped Joan could see it in the reflected firelight because it had her name on it. Then he again addressed his congregated fellow strandees. "Listen up, everyone. My real name is Dan Hendricks, and I'm a deputy sheriff of Taos County. Mark, verify this, please."

Again Mark called out, "He's telling the truth. I've known him since we were kids. He's not crazy, either. Well, not as crazy as you were led to believe."

Repeated murmurs had Dan rolling his eyes. "Thanks, buddy. Now, here's what's going to happen, ladies and gentlemen. You're all going to stay here where you can be accounted for. Look around, see who's missing. I'm going to need names. Mark, you check the circuit box and have your people get flashlights, candles, whatever we can use for light. And someone keep the fire going in here."

"You got it, Dan. But the emergency generator's outside. I'll need to get my coat and go check it, see why it's not up and running. It might've been tampered with."

Mark's assessment renewed the fearful whisperings in the room. Dan huffed out a breath. "Okay, but get me a coat, too. I don't want you going out there alone."

"I don't want me too, either," Mark assured him. In the next second, his footsteps could be heard crossing the flagstones. His voice carried as he called his employees to him and assigned them tasks to carry out Dan's orders.

Just when Dan thought everything was under control, from another corner of the room came, "Hey, young fella, you need any help? I'm armed, and I'm your man."

"Oh, for pity's sake, Julius. You most certainly are not anybody's man—except mine. Other than that, you're an old codger on vacation."

And that would be Ethel, the missus. Dan grinned into the darkness, answering, "Thanks, Mr. Garrison, but she's right. You're a civilian. I can't involve you. And why are you armed?"

"Not to worry. I'm licensed to carry. Armed and primed, I am. Already got mine in my hand. I expect it's bigger than yours, got more notches on it. Been around longer, that's for sure. May as well put it to good use before it quits working on me altogether."

A tug on his jeans had Dan looking down at Joan, who whispered, "We are still talking about guns, aren't we?"

Dan huffed out his breath. "I sure as hell hope so." Then he called out, "I'd be happy for the help, Mr. Garrison, as long as you understand the risks. Just move over here by me, toward the fireplace. The rest of you, take a head count.'' As they set about obeying, Dan watched the crowd alertly to make sure *only* Mr. Garrison separated himself from the throng.

He did. To Dan's relief, the older man indeed clutched in his hand a gun. And only a gun. When the gutsy old gentleman stopped in front of him, Dan spoke so only he could hear him. ''I'm thinking this power outage is deliberate. What's your take?''

The rumpled little man raised his wicked-looking, long-barreled pistol— *Yep, bigger'n mine,* Dan conceded—and began checking it over as he said, ''I take it you're right. If it was the snow's weight, this would've happened yesterday.'' Then he added, ''This happenin' because of Miss O'Leary here?''

Wide-eyed with watching the crusty New Englander's fumbling, arthritic hands all but mishandle such a powerful weapon, Dan at first missed the man's words. Then the old guy's conclusion caught up with Dan's hearing. He jerked his head up, met Mr. Garrison's steady gaze. ''How'd you know she's—''

''Joan O'Leary? Seen her picture in the papers a while back. She's the one arrested for that LoBianco murder. I told the missus I thought I recognized her. But don't worry none—I kept it to myself. Except for the missus.''

Dan could only stare. Then he accused, ''You're like someone else I know. You don't miss a thing, do you?''

Something blunt kicked Dan's booted ankle. He grunted, suspecting it was the toe of Joan's shoe. He looked down at her, but immediately shot his gaze to Mr. Garrison when the man directed a question her way. ''You didn't kill that mob fella, did you, young lady?''

First, silence met his query. Dan's expression went grim. Then, "No, I didn't, Mr. Garrison."

Dan exhaled and then recaptured the older man's attention. "Try to keep everyone calm. Make them stay here. But especially keep an eye on Miss O'Leary for me. And please, don't shoot yourself or anybody else with that cannon."

Mr. Garrison nodded. "Never have shot anybody yet that didn't need it. Now, after you check that generator with your friend, what's your next move? I'd hate for you to just pop back in and surprise me, causing me to ruin my clean shootin' record."

"Yeah, I'd hate that, too," Dan retorted, frowning as he ran a hand over his jaw and took in Joan's anxious expression. Better keep his next move to himself. He turned back to his pistol-packin' deputy. "I'll be right back inside after we check the emergency power."

Mr. Garrison nodded, mimicking Dan by rubbing his gnarly-fingered hand over his stubbly jaw. "That's one way. But if it was me, I'd be hunting who it was who just left and finding out why he did. But I'd already know it was the real murderer and that he meant to draw me out, to get rid of me so he can get her."

"Thanks," Dan deadpanned. "Now she's really going to—"

Joan jumped up and clutched him. "Dan, you cannot go out there. Please. Don't do this."

"Worry," he finished to Mr. Garrison. Then he turned to Joan, gently gripping her arm with his free hand. "I can't let Mark go out there alone. No more than I can allow whoever's out there to get tired of waiting for me and come in shooting. Look around. I've got a roomful of innocent, helpless people. What would you have me do—sit on my hands?"

Her grip on him tightened, but she shook her head no as tears sprang to her eyes. In the next moment, she rested her forehead against his chest. Dan smoothed his hand over her hair, kissing the top of her head. She pulled back, raising a tear-stained face to him. "Be careful."

A tenderness he'd never before experienced claimed Dan's spirit. He smiled at her, smoothing his knuckles across her soft cheeks as he wiped away her tears and said, for her ears only, "I will. It's going to be okay, Joan. Do you believe me this time?"

She lowered her gaze, but again she nodded. "I do."

Dan tucked a finger under her chin and urged her to raise her head, to look into his eyes. "Good." So much conveyed with so few words. Dan couldn't believe it. And yet, he was beginning to believe. In himself. In Joan. In what was between them, and tugging them together.

Just then, footsteps reentering the lobby caught everyone's attention. In no more than a split second, Dan had Joan turned away from the possible danger and his gun aimed in that direction. Mr. Garrison stood stiffly at his side, his gun also leveled at the intruders. A grim smile of respect for the old guy's courage crossed Dan's features. He then called out, "We've got you covered. Stop and identify yourselves."

The footsteps stopped. "It's us, Dan. We got the coats and the other stuff, like you said."

Dan wilted with relief and turned it to vexation. "Dammit, Mark, I almost shot you. Just wait there. I'll come to you."

So, all was in readiness. There was nothing left to do but to do it. Dan exhaled, ignored the tightness in his chest, and again looked at Joan, memorizing her face. Then he kissed her and turned to Mr. Garrison. "You're in charge."

The older man nodded, saying, "We'll be fine. You just

watch yourself out there. Wouldn't want you to get eaten by a bear.''

Dan's chuckle joined Joan's, watery as hers was. He winked at her, and made a mental note to tell Mr. Garrison one day why that was so funny.

JOAN WATCHED Dan's retreating figure, never taking her gaze off him as he donned the heavy coat Mark handed him, never glancing away as he headed for the lodge's front doors around the corner. She even remained staring at the empty space he'd just occupied, until she heard the doors hiss open, and close behind him. Then she rounded on Mr. Garrison. "I'm not going to sit here while he's out there alone. We've got to do something.''

"And we will, Miss O'Leary.'' With that, he turned on his heel, put two fingers to his mouth and pierced the air with a high-pitched, eardrum-popping whistle that made Joan's teeth itch. An immediate hush settled over the room, all heads turned his way. "All right, you know your assignments,'' he called out. "It's time. Battle stations!''

Joan had time only to mouth *Battle stations?* before flashlights flicked on, lighting the crowded room like Hollywood spotlights on Oscar night. Murky shadows moved restlessly about, seemingly at random. Then they sorted themselves out, became familiar old folks, all of whom came up with coats and—shock of the century—guns. Of every make and model and year since the advent of gunpowder, it seemed to Joan's untrained eye.

Joan grabbed Mr. Garrison's wiry arm, capturing his attention. "What in the name of all that's holy is going on?''

"We're going to help your young man. I lied to him about not telling anyone who you are. I told everyone who you are. And we feel just terrible for you. We knew you couldn't have done it, a nice girl like you. So when that Mark fella said the snowplows are coming through tomorrow, we feared the real killer would try something tonight. So we came up with a plan—''

''You know about the hit man? How?''

''I didn't. Just thought like he did and figured out what I'd do in his place.''

Joan stared at him. ''Who are you—I mean, really?''

''Julius J. Garrison, brigadier general, U.S. Air Force, retired. And so's everyone else here. Retired military, that is. We all kept our ranks and formed a gun club to travel together. Go on maneuvers. Take part in war games. It's not much, but it keeps us active.''

Joan absorbed his words, still staring at him. ''And your plan?''

''Well, after we got you to leave the meeting today, we ironed out the details. Now, here's what we—''

Joan jerked her hand up. ''There's no 'we' to it. There's just me. And I'm going outside—with a gun you're going to give me.'' Joan looked from the man to his elderly, armed-to-the-teeth geriatric army, and back to him. No one offered her a gun. ''Give me your gun, and don't try to stop me.''

''Didn't plan on it,'' the retired general chirped as he gripped her arm and escorted her through the crowd, which melted back at their approach and then stepped along smartly behind them. Across the lobby they doddered. Why did she suddenly feel railroaded? Joan wondered as she peeked repeatedly over her shoulder.

When they drew even with Mrs. Compton, that sweet little dear hoisted a lethal-looking old musket onto her shoulder and smiled. Plopping her flashlight in Joan's hand, she said, ''Major Edna Compton here, dear. Take this. You'll need it. It's dark upstairs.''

Major? Upstairs? Joan stared at the device as if it had simply materialized in her grip, and then mumbled ''Thanks'' over her shoulder as Mr.—General Garrison resumed her forced march to the darkened stairwell. Once there, he said, "Get your coat. We'll wait here. We'd just slow you down."

Joan nodded as if she understood what was going on. She flicked on the light, gripped the handrail attached to the stucco wall and pretended she was still in charge. "Okay, I guess we're in this together. You *better* wait for me."

"We will," he assured her with a curt nod. Several others flanking him also murmured their assurances. Mr. Garrison added, "You're our bait."

Joan's chin dipped down. "Say that again."

General Garrison repeated, "Our bait. For the hit man."

Her chin dipped farther. "There is no part of what you just said that I like."

"I suppose not. Now, go and get your coat. There's not much time."

Thus urged, Joan took a step, but immediately stopped when the muted *pop-pop-pop* of outside gunfire sounded, and had them all staring at each other. "Dan!" Joan shouted as she tried to get past the army blocking her way. Two old men looped her waist with surprisingly strong grips and halted her. "Let me go," she cried. "I have to help him."

General Garrison gripped her shoulders. "How? By rushin' out there and gettin' yourself shot? Listen to me—that was his gun you heard. So your Dan is doing the shootin'. That means he's alive. Now hurry along. Let's see if we can keep him that way."

Joan recovered and jerked around, pulling away from him and leaping up the steep stairs. "Where will you be?" she called over her shoulder.

"I'll be postin' guards and checkin' all the exits. Be careful up there."

"I will," Joan yelled back, leading with the flashlight's

beam as she rounded the landing and flew up to the second floor and then the third. Finally on the fourth floor, she flashed her light ahead of her, didn't see anybody and quick-stepped her way to her door. There, she tucked the flashlight up under her arm and shoved her hand in her jeans' front pocket, searching for and finding her room keys.

Shaky with fear and from her flight, she needed three fumbling attempts to get the dead-bolted door open. Finally, she succeeded and lurched inside, where she swept the darkened room with the flashlight's narrow beam until it showed her the quilted orange coat draped over that pink chair by the closet. "Yes!" she muttered, striding stiff-legged to it and snatching up the coat.

Now she could get outside and help Dan. She jerked around—and came near to dying of muscle-locking fright right then and there. Because she'd just caught in her beam of light a short, heavyset man.

Too late she realized she hadn't closed the door behind her. The man's almost comical face, when unevenly high-lighted like this, gave him the appearance of a spook-house phantom. Standing not twenty feet from her and silent as a tomb, he took another step her way. The lenses of his black-rimmed eyeglasses reflected her battery-powered light and hid his eyes.

Groucho. Joan went weak with relief, but grimaced her exasperation. "Look, you have really bad timing here. I'm flattered by your attention, but in case you haven't noticed, we're all involved in a life-or-death—"

"Yeah, yours. On both counts." His voice—it wasn't the gravelly one he'd used at the sing-along. But where had she heard his real one? It was familiar. He shoved up a sleeve of his turtleneck sweater, revealing on his fore-arm...a tattoo of a native chieftain in full headdress.

Joan's eyes widened, her heart pounded. She shook her head, whimpering, "You. You killed Mr. LoBianco."

He shrugged. "It was business." And removed his glasses, tossing them aside, then peeling off the fake eyebrows and mustache, which he flicked away, too. Revealed now was a broad, craggy face, like a bulldog's. He pulled from his waistband a really big gun, which he pointed at her. "Sorry I gotta do this. You're a nice girl and all. But you're just too smart."

"No, you're wrong," Joan blurted. "I'm actually very stupid."

"No, you ain't—you figured out Tony's numbers was all wrong. See, I went through them books you dropped. Not that I was in Taos to check up on you. I was supposed to off Tony before he ratted out the boss to the cops. But Tony begged, said I could have the money he'd skimmed if I'd let him disappear. I said how much money. He said he didn't know because you had the books."

Figuring as long as he was talking, she was breathing, Joan kept up her end. "So...you waited for me to show up?"

"Yeah. But then Tony got wise that I was going to keep the money *and* kill him. And you, too. He went nuts, said you was an innocent, said I wasn't goin' to touch you. Then he came at me with his own knife. I had to kill him."

A tremor of guilt and sadness shook her. Mr. LoBianco, a mobster and murderer and all-around rat-fink, had died trying to protect *her* life? The shock...she couldn't absorb it. She stared helplessly at her would-be assassin. "And then I came along and saw you do it."

"Yeah, so I couldn't leave you alive. The boss wouldn't be none too happy. I guess you should've called in sick that night, Miss O'Leary. 'Cause now...I gotta kill you."

11

THIS IS WHAT I NEED, Dan fumed. He knelt on one knee in the dirty snow behind the Dumpster. *A turkey-shoot of a showdown with the mob—while it's pitch-black night and freezing cold. Oh, and over there? A lodge full of helpless old folks and the woman I just might love.* Thus…buoyed, Dan scooted forward to peer cautiously around the smelly bin's cold metal side.

''Whoo-whoo.''

Dan jerked around, tensing to keep from firing at the first thing that moved. Then his brain identified the sound for him. *Owl.* Dan shook his head as he exhaled his flash of fright and again turned toward the black hulk of the lodge, which jutted out of the mountain, resembling a ship plowing through a high sea. He then cut his gaze to the parking lot, seeing only a big tour bus, a few cars and surrounding them all, the overcast darkness, unrelieved by moonlight.

Come on, show your face, Dan silently urged his unseen adversary, the one whose bullet had almost taken his head off a minute ago. Lucky for him, he'd also missed Mark who'd just sprinted, under cover of Dan's fire, back to the safety of the lodge. Dan tried not to think about where the gangster might be this minute. Because he feared he knew. Inside. Where Joan was. And all those old folks. Talk about your nightmares. But since he couldn't be sure, couldn't just stick his neck out to find out, here he was. Stuck outside until he could work his own way back to the lodge.

What he wouldn't give for a minute of moonlight to show him his quarry. But no. Dan gritted his jaw and tried to stay so still he could maybe hear the mobster. *Probably right behind me, the way my last few days have gone.* Not that the thought spooked him, but he jerked around again, wagging his 9-mm from left to right.

Only to find himself...alone. *Whew.* Okay, so the hit man wasn't on his butt. Check that off his list of possible hiding places. Dan pushed up to his feet, crouching low but working his muscles lest they become sluggish from the cold. All his training said to keep moving around, give the enemy a mobile target, make him show his position. *And use yourself as bait.*

Dan silently counted to three—*hook, line, sinker*—and then slouched away from the overhanging pine branches and the Dumpster's squat body. Hustling forward, crunching snow underfoot, he headed for the two-story-high forest of treated-wood beams that staked the lodge's decking. Half expecting to feel the white-hot bite of a bullet slam into him at any moment, he didn't risk even a breath until he'd achieved the relative shelter of the rows of milled trunks.

Once there, and breathing hard, listening, adjusting his vision, he jammed a shoulder against a pillar. And snapped to rigid attention. There. Above him, on the topside deck...Dan got his bearings...in front of the ski-equipment store. Had he heard footsteps? Dan swallowed, swiped sweat out of his eyes, looked straight up, and two-handedly raised his gun along with his gaze. *Got you, you murdering son of a bitch.*

GROUCHO'S DARK EYES and grease-slickened black hair glinted in Joan's beam of light as he took a step toward her. She knew she should move, run, dodge, do something. But tell that to her feet. They'd grown roots. Therefore, her last moments on Earth would apparently be spent shining her little light on her murderer. That visual finally unlocked her muscles and her brain. *So why am I making it easier for him? I don't have time for this. Dan's life is in danger.*

Duh. She flicked off her flashlight, plunging the room into blackness as she leaped for the bed. Groucho cursed, fired at where she'd been, and missed. Joan hit the mattress with such force that a yelp escaped her as she bounced onto her back and lost the flashlight, her only weapon.

Then suddenly the man's weight was atop her, all but crushing her, forcing her breath out in a *whoosh*. Grunting, straining, he grappled with her, trying to grab her arms and pin them above her head. Having to fight her long hair and him, Joan twisted and elbowed and gouged, finally gaining one hand free of his grip. She flung it back, away from his clawing fingers, only to whack the heavy table lamp above her head.

Like a bowling pin hit low, it flew forward, missing Joan but catching Groucho's head. It broke over his skull, thus nobly sacrificing itself, and rendering Groucho dead weight atop Joan. For one unreasoning second, she lay there among the lamp shards, under her attacker, blinking and numbly contemplating the funnel-shaped shade that now perched like a coolie hat on Groucho's head.

But in the next second, she became a blur of panicked limbs as she freed herself of the man and scooted off the bed. Two giant steps and she was across the room, her back and palms plastered against the wall. Breathing hard, she stared at him. *Maybe you ought to get out of here.* Right. Another flurry of motion, and Joan had the flashlight and her coat. She spared the man another glance. He hadn't moved. But could.

So, get out. Still a good idea. She jerked around, cutting and running for the relative safety of the hallway, down which she scampered, and really flew when she heard a growl of noise, jerked around, saw Groucho stumbling out of the room, gun in hand. Joan screeched and took the stairs in a stumbling, tumbling run down to the lobby. "Mr. Garrison!" she called as she went. "Help me! Groucho's after me!"

Downstairs, white-haired heads turned her way. General Garrison separated himself from the group, came toward her. Joan flung herself into his embrace, noting the startlement on his face. Scared, shaking in reaction to her ordeal, she hugged him fiercely and cried out, "The hit man. It's Groucho. He has the tattoo and those were fake eyebrows and stuff. He tried to kill me, but the lamp attacked him and then I—"

Mr. Garrison pulled her back by the arms and brushed her hair back from her hot, damp face. "The lamp… attacked Groucho?"

She jerked her gaze up to the stairs. Empty. So far. "Yes. Up there. Hurry. We have to get him. Give me a gun. Quick." A brief pause. "Why are you looking at me like that?"

OUTSIDE, a sudden break in the clouds revealed the moon's light and silvered Dan's surroundings. Loading a fresh clip into his Beretta, he glanced up at the moon in gratitude and reconsidered his position. Standing with his back to the parking lot, his hip abutting the wooden railing of the broad steps that led to the deck above, and his eyes narrowed in concentration, he glanced this way and that, and— *What the hell is that?*

Immediately he ducked to one side of the railing. He'd seen something…a movement. At the head of the stairs closest to the lodge. A shadow. He chanced another peek, saw nothing, and straightened up. He was losing it. Shaking his head, Dan lowered his gaze to check—only to pop his head right back up, like a jack-in-the-box. *What the—?* Apparently, he wasn't losing it, because there it—they?—were again.

They? If he didn't know better…Dan rubbed his eyes, looked again…he'd say there was a band of old geezers, all of them armed to the teeth, coming toward him. *Oh, sweet Georgia Brown. I have a posse. Right out in the open.* His insides, blood and guts and all, curdled. Sighing, certain the world had gone mad, leaving him the only sane person left, Dan stepped into the moonlight, very cautiously, and stage-whispered, "Pssst. Over here. Don't shoot. It's me. What in the hell are you doing out here?"

"Is that you, Deputy?" some old dude called out. Dan's knees stiffened against the fear that a shot would ring out and find any one of them at any moment. "Sergeant Akins here. We were sent out to get you. We got him. Or Miss O'Leary did."

Sergeant? Got who? God, he didn't want to ask. Dan swiped a hand over his frozen jaw, huffed out his warm breath and asked, "Got who?"

The answer was a long time coming, but finally, "Why, that there gangster hit man, of course. Who'd you think?"

Dan's knees buckled. He clutched at the stair railing. "Did you say Miss O'Leary got him?" It was happening again. He hadn't been there to help the woman he loved, to save her.

A throat was cleared at the top of the stairs. Whispering ensued. Then, "Yes. Only sort of got him, though."

Sort of? Then, this wasn't over. There was still time. Dan muttered a curse not fit for print and sprinted up the stairs, or as near to sprinting as he could get, what with his legs not wanting to support his weight. At the top of the stairs now, he looked at what faced him. And his heart nearly stopped. Thousand-year-old men and women with even older guns. He'd sort this out later. For now, Joan was uppermost in his mind. "Where exactly is Miss O'Leary?"

"Right here." Dan jerked to his right, looked over the heads surrounding him. Loud and clear, his New England tones ringing through the crisp night air, Mr. Garrison held up his gun hand and chirped, "She's right here, young fella. I didn't let her out of my sight. Well, except for when she went to get her coat and Groucho attacked her."

Attacked—? Dan's knees gave. "Joan!" Several hands reached for him.

Then Joan was in his arms, her arms around his waist, her hands fisted around his coat, her cheek against his chest. "I was so scared, Dan. Are you all right?"

Dan inhaled, mouth open, eyes closed, and felt his heart begin to beat again. Joan was alive. His world was complete. Then he grabbed her arms and pulled her back so he could look into the only face he'd ever want to see lying on the pillow next to his every morning for the rest of his life. Then, careful of his gun, he ran his other hand over her face, across her shoulder, down her arm. "Am I all right? What about you? Are you hurt anywhere? Did he hurt you?"

"No," she said, shaking her head. "He just tackled me on the bed, but then the lamp attacked him, stunning him. And I got away. But then he chased me down the hall—"

"Joan, honey, where is he now? Groucho. Where is he?" God, he didn't want to hear this answer.

"I don't know."

Which was why he hadn't wanted to hear her answer. "You don't know?" He looked up, searched his posse's suddenly sheepish-looking faces. "You don't know, either, do you?"

"Can't say that we do," Mr. Garrison informed him,

scratching at his wispy-white hair under his knit ski cap. "That Mark fella came in about the time Miss O'Leary came running down and said he had that emergency generator's diesel engine up and going. We elected not to chase the hit man down in the dark upstairs, so we came out here. Can't really say where he is right this minute, though. Could be out here, I suppose. But Mark's inside now going through all the fuses. Should have some light on the subject here in a minute. Ought to make a search easier."

"Yeah. Ought to," Dan replied dryly. "So, why are we standing around out here in moonlight, like sitting ducks? Anybody?"

Apparently, no one wanted to field that question. Silence rained down like icicles. Dan sighed out his breath, spared his surroundings another once-over—*stupid assassin must be in Taos by now if he hasn't opened fire yet*—and stared across the upper parking lot. They needed to get out of this moonlight before—

Blink. Siz-z-le. Wink. Fo-o-op!

The electric lights blazed on in a show of modern technological glory. Daytime. High noon. Sunshine bright. Dan froze, his breath caught. He heard similar gasps around him, felt Joan's hold on him tighten, and looked down at her. Her face was contorted with fear. Suddenly she wrenched away from him, pushed him backward, yelled, "Dan, look out!"

Stumbling backward to the edge of the deck, Dan couldn't look out, but Mr. Garrison hollered, "Holy moly! Duck, young fella!" Dan ducked, hit the snow, covered his head. In the next millisecond, antique guns were ready-aim-fired. Smoky booms and pings and whizzes of gunfire airplaned over Dan's head and thudded into the snow somewhere behind him.

"Son of a—!" When he'd fallen to the ground, Dan's

gun had flown from his hand to slide right over the edge of the deck. "Cease fire, dammit! Cease fire! What the hell's the matter with you?"

The firing stopped. All was quiet. Dan raised his head, looked up, saw Joan rush to him, with Garrison's raiders close behind. Frowning, Dan wrenched over, stared at the lit-up parking lot below him and nearly passed out.

On his feet and reaching for the sky, his automatic rifle on the ground in front of him, was…Groucho. And he hadn't been hit, not even once. Amazing. But obviously, since he'd laid down his weapon, the posse had made their point. A grin, a chuckle, and Dan had the hit man's panicked attention.

The stocky guy pointed to the army behind Dan and yelled, "Make 'em stop, lawman. Don't let them get me. Call 'em off."

Now, that was funny. And Dan laughed to prove it. "Call them off? I don't think so. They'll be right with you. And my advice to you is…don't move."

At that moment, Joan skidded into him, slid down on her bottom right beside him and grabbed him around the neck, crying. "I thought you were dead. You scared me. Don't you ever do that again. Don't you know that I love you?"

"Shh. I love you, too. I'm fine. It's okay. I told you it would be." Dan wrapped his arms around her, hugging her fiercely to him, burying his face in her thick, fragrant hair. She felt so good. So right.

And for the first time, despite all the times he'd said it to her, Dan really could believe that they would be okay.

"NO! NOT YET." Still breathing erratically, her skin dewy from lovemaking, Joan clung to Dan's naked shoulders, not wanting him to roll off her, not yet. She just wanted to look at him in the bright light of the next day. With the room's curtains open, a stray morning beam shyly crossed the room to backlight him, to glint off his black hair and bask them both in a warm glow. This moment, their world was perfect.

"What's wrong?" Dan grinned as he settled his weight atop her in a most delicious way, and kissed the tip of her nose.

Joan's breath caught in a gasping response to his hips' movement against hers. But still she managed a pout. "What's wrong? The snow's melting. And the plows are clearing the roads outside, even as we...speak. And the phones are back on. You just had to call work, didn't you? How many times has it rung since? Ten, maybe? I want you to myself. Don't you understand?"

Dan stared down at her, his expression as serious as the charges against Groucho, who was secured downstairs in the utility closet—and guarded by...General Garrison's retired army. "I understand more than you know. I feel as though I have died and gone to heaven, and you are my reward."

Joan chuckled and shoved at his arm. Dan grinned and rolled off her—despite her renewed protests. He held a hand up as if taking an oath. "I'm not going anywhere again, I swear it."

To prove it, he scooted next to her, on his side, his elbow propped against the sheets, his head supported in his palm. With his other hand, he sketched sensuous circles on her naked belly as he explained, "Okay, *A*—no more calls to work. But *B*—you should be glad I did call, because *C*—Sheriff Halverson says the D.A. is dropping the charges against you. And *D*—"

Joan covered his mouth with her palm. "And *D*—your boss said for you to place me under your protective custody as a federal witness against the assassin downstairs. I know."

His hazel eyes sparking mischief, Dan licked her palm, causing her to squeal and jerk it away, but he caught it and put it right back to his mouth, kissed her palm, and then held her hand in his, against his chest. "And is that not exactly where you've been ever since? Under me?"

Rolling her eyes at his male smugness, Joan half-heartedly tried, but completely failed, to free her hand from his possessive grip. "Do you hear yourself? You are some piece of work, Dan—"

A loud *rap-rap-rap* on the room's locked door cut off her words and spooked them into looking that way, even as they groaned their protest. "There's nobody here. Go away," Dan yelled as he winked at her. No reply from the hallway. He shrugged his shoulders. "That was easy."

Joan nodded, but too soon. Again, the knocking. She raised her eyebrows in question. Dan frowned and cocked his head, suddenly intent, suddenly the lawman, as he eyed the door and called out, "State your business."

After a moment's hesitation, a voice thick with an East Coast accent, answered, "Mr. Giovanelli would like a word with the lady, Deputy Hendricks. A quick social call, nothing more."

Dan's eyes widened, scaring Joan with the implications. She clutched his arm. "Who's Mr. Giovanelli?" she asked.

Dan looked from the door to her. "He's Groucho's and Tony LoBianco's boss."

"Oh, my God," Joan breathed. "What do you think he wants with me?"

Dan's raised eyebrows wrinkled his forehead. "You have to ask? Get up, get your clothes and lock yourself in the bathroom. And don't open it for anyone but me. You got that?"

Biting her bottom lip, Joan nodded, but a repeated *rap-rap-rap* against the door startled them into stillness and wide-eyed staring at each other. The same voice called out, "Mr. Giovanelli doesn't like being kept waiting."

Dan's expression soured. Joan gripped his arm and shook her head vigorously in a silent plea, which Dan ignored to call out, "And I don't like being bothered when I'm in bed. So he'll just have to wait a damned minute." Then he whispered to her, "You can't show fear to these guys. And I'm the law here."

"Well, just inscribe that on my headstone, Sheriff," Joan whispered, her stomach already sinking like the Titanic.

It really thudded to the ocean floor when another voice out in the hall, one she recognized all too well—General Garrison's—offered, "We could break down the door, if you like."

"No, wait!" Joan called out, eliciting a hiss of protest from Dan. She dug her fingernails into his forearm to keep him silent. "Just let us get dressed. Please." And then they waited.

In the next second, they heard, "Two minutes."

Dan narrowed his eyes at the door and pulled her off the bed with him. Together, like the least intelligent of rats negotiating a maze, they raced around the room, gathering up their clothes and colliding at every turn. Finally, Dan, now in his boxers and T-shirt, grabbed his denims, danced into them and buttoned the fly. Joan settled her little-children-of-the-world sweater over her head in time to see Dan grab his Beretta and work the safety and then the slide. He looked over at her as he tucked it—in plain sight—in his waistband. "You do know that I'm duty-bound to arrest this man?"

Joan fisted her hands at her waist. "Well, you're not gonna." She looked down at herself. Barefoot, jeans, sweater. Decent. She raked her fingers through her hair and scrunched her bangs. "I'm not hiding in the bathroom.

Open the door." Dan's mouth turned down, but he gripped the doorknob. "Dan?"

He turned to her, a question in his frowning expression.

"I love you. There'll be another day for you with this guy."

Dan eyed her a moment and then winked as he quirked his mouth into a grin. "You're right. I'm letting pride get in the way. The federal case against him is shot to hell with LoBianco dead. But watch this guy separate himself from the knucklehead in the utility closet."

Joan all but wilted with relief that Dan would be reasonable—and, therefore, safe. She watched him unlock the dead bolt and call out to the people in the hall. "You can come in, nice and slow. Just Mr. Giovanelli. I'm armed, and I have you covered, so don't try anything funny."

"I'm comin' in with him, son," the general called out. "I'm armed, so there won't be any trouble. Mr. Giovanelli just wants to thank Miss O'Leary in person, and then he's gone."

Dan arrowed her a questioning look—*You want to do this?* She shrugged—*Do we have a choice?* Dan gave her an answering shrug and opened the door, revealing two really big, handsome businessmen-looking guys in expensive black wool overcoats who shouldered in front of a short, balding, older man of slight build. And General Garrison.

This third man and the general elbowed their way between the two human pillars and stepped into the room. Mr. Giovanelli turned to his escorts. "Wait here," he instructed them. They did, but they looked as though they didn't like it. Then the man closed the door, turned to Dan, nodded and came toward Joan. The closer he got, the wider her eyes opened, the more she twisted her fingers together.

In cartoonish quickness, Dan was at her side before the mob boss was.

Again he eyed Dan, sliding his gaze to the Beretta poking out of his pants, and then he offered a well-manicured hand and a smile to Joan. "Miss O'Leary, I'm Gino Giovanelli. I just wanted to tell you how grateful I am for everything you've done for me."

Dan jostled her shoulder, prompting her to take the man's hand—it was warm, his grip firm—and shake it. "You're welcome, but I don't know what you think I've done—"

"You saved me—" he eyed Dan "—a lot of money, Miss O'Leary. That's important to a businessman such as myself." He smiled, a very charming, sincere expression. "It was a good thing Tony did...dying for you like that. A very good thing. I hated finding out he was gone, done in by my own employee—" again he eyed Dan "—who was acting on his own. It hurts me, right here." He thumped his fist over his heart. "But you? Look at you. A smart girl. And pretty. You ever need a job, you look me up."

Résumé entry: Accountant to the Mob. Joan swallowed, tried to smile, didn't feel she was succeeding. "I'll remember that."

He nodded. "Good. You do that." Then he turned to Dan, addressing him directly. "This closes your case, eh, Deputy?"

Joan saw the muscle tic in Dan's jaw. She held her breath, waited for his answer and heard him say, "It does. For now."

The mob boss nodded. "For now." Then he turned to Joan again, adding, "You're one of ours now. Anyone gives you any trouble, don't worry about it. We'll keep an eye on you—"

"That's...*really* not necessary." She clutched Dan's arm. "I'll be fine."

Gino Giovanelli took it all in and grinned, pointing from her to Dan and back to her. "So you two got a thing going, yeah? That's good. That's real good. I like that. I'm a sucker for a good romance, a happy ending and all. Two kids in love, making a life together. When you have your babies, you name the first boy Gino, eh? I'll see he has everything he needs—all his life."

Joan's eyes widened to the point of pain. She shook her head no, got bumped by Dan and blurted, "Oh, um, that's...that's very kind of you."

"Yeah, it is kind, isn't it? I like that." Then he roused himself, turned a steely game-of-nerves look on Dan, but offered his hand, which Dan finally shook. Then the mob kingpin said, "You got a good girl here. Anything bad happens to her, you'll answer to me." Giving Dan no chance for a response, he turned to Joan, gripped her shoulders and pulled her to him for a quick kiss on her cheek. "You, I like. Have a good life, Joan O'Leary."

And then he turned, strode confidently across the room, opened the door, never looking back, and was gone. Leaving General Garrison to join Dan and Joan in staring at the closed door. For long, quiet moments. Then, Joan turned to Dan, saying, "Wow. I thought we were dead. I can't believe we pulled that one off."

Dan cut his gaze over to her. "Yeah, talk about escaping with your life. Imagine—Gino Giovanelli. Right here in this room."

Joan grinned. "Yeah. And he likes me. He wants me to have a good life, too. You better make sure I get it, Sheriff."

"Which is where I and this shotgun come in."

Joan turned with Dan to stare at the older man. "Okay, I'll bite," Dan said.

"This afternoon, two o'clock, down in the lobby, there's going to be a wedding. Yours. Can't have you children living in sin another day. I'm officiating. Licenses and all can come later. So don't be late."

"A wedding? Ours?" Joan looked up at Dan. "A wedding?"

Dan turned to her, his frown knitting vertical lines between his eyes. He crossed his arms over his chest. "You heard the man. And he has a gun. So, what do you say?"

"You asking?" Joan breathed, afraid to believe.

"Yep. And you better say yes. Because I have enough problems, as it is. Our federal case was just blown out of the water. We still have the election to think about. My grandfather's got some lady with child and has invited all of Taos to his wedding. On Halloween. Shep's got some collie with puppies. And—"

"Yes. And I want you to give me your baby."

"And you want me to—" Dan stopped, lowered his arms to his side, his face lighting with a happy emotion. "Yes? You will?" Then he frowned. "We're not naming it Gino. Gino Hendricks? I don't think so."

Giddy with happiness but playing along with Dan's mock seriousness, Joan agreed, "Of course not. Gino O'Leary-Hendricks. Hyphenated."

Dan looked from her, to the grinning general, and back to her. "A hyphenated name? That ought to get his little butt kicked every day on the playground."

"Not if the mob is guarding him. Aren't I right, General Garrison?"

"Ah-yep," he responded. "I'll just leave you two kids alone for now. See you at two. Dress in your best. Everyone will be there.'' With that, he executed a sharp about-face, marched to the door and left.

Joan looked back to Dan in time to see him skirt her and go to the bed. Once there, he jerked up the wilted bedspread from the floor and revealed his boots, which he picked up.

''What are you doing? Where are you going?''

Dan sat on the end of the bed and began tugging his boots on. He flicked his hazel-eyed gaze to her and then concentrated on his task. ''Since I'm apparently not going to be needing all those condoms, I'm going to get a refund on the unused ones. We've got about eight thousand of 'em in this room.''

Joan shrieked and launched herself at him, shoving him backward onto the bed and holding him there. ''We do not. And you are not, Dan Hendricks! I would be so embarrassed—''

''Right...Barbie.'' His arms went around her. ''Now cuddle up to your Ken and let's see about making a baby doll.'' And he kissed her deeply.

LOVE & LAUGHTER™

SEXY COWBOYS.
SASSY WOMEN. LOVE ON THE RANCH.

**Don't miss these entertaining
cowboy stories...**

May 1998
#43 THERE GOES THE BRIDE
Renee Roszel

June 1998
#46 HOW THE WEST WAS WED
Jule McBride

July 1998
#48 COUNTERFEIT COWGIRL
Lois Greiman

August 1998
#50 GETTIN' LUCKY
Kimberly Raye

Stetsons, spurs and sparks make great
romantic comedy.

Available wherever Harlequin books are sold.

Take 4 bestselling love stories FREE

a FREE surprise gift!

Special Limited-time Offer

Mail to Harlequin Reader Service®

3010 Walden Avenue
P.O. Box 1867
Buffalo, N.Y. 14240-1867

YES! Please send me 4 free Harlequin Love and Laughter™ novels and my free surprise gift. Then send me 4 brand-new novels every other month, which I will receive months before they appear in bookstores. Bill me at the low price of $2.90 each plus 25¢ delivery per book and applicable sales tax if any*. That's the complete price and a savings of over 10% off the cover prices— quite a bargain! I understand that accepting the books and gift places me under no obligation ever to buy any books. I can always return a shipment and cancel at any time. Even if I never buy another book from Harlequin, the 4 free books and the surprise gift are mine to keep forever.

102 BPA A7EF

Name	(PLEASE PRINT)	
Address		Apt. No.
City	State	Zip

This offer is limited to one order per household and not valid to present Love and Laughter™ subscribers. *Terms and prices are subject to change without notice. Sales tax applicable in N.Y.

ULL-397

©1996 Harlequin Enterprises Limited

Catch more great

HARLEQUIN™ Movies

featured on the movie channel tmc

Premiering May 9th
The Awakening

starring Cynthia Geary and
David Beecroft, based on the novel by
Patricia Coughlin

Don't miss next month's movie!
Premiering June 13th
Diamond Girl
based on the novel by bestselling author
Diana Palmer

If you are not currently a subscriber to
The Movie Channel, simply call your
local cable or satellite provider for more
details. Call today, and don't miss out
on the romance!

Don't miss these Harlequin favorites by some of our bestselling authors!

HT#25721	THE ONLY MAN IN WYOMING	$3.50 U.S.	☐
	by Kristine Rolofson	$3.99 CAN.	☐
HP#11869	WICKED CAPRICE	$3.50 U.S.	☐
	by Anne Mather	$3.99 CAN.	☐
HR#03438	ACCIDENTAL WIFE	$3.25 U.S.	☐
	by Day Leclaire	$3.75 CAN.	☐
HS#70737	STRANGERS WHEN WE MEET	$3.99 U.S.	☐
	by Rebecca Winters	$4.50 CAN.	☐
HI#22405	HERO FOR HIRE	$3.75 U.S.	☐
	by Laura Kenner	$4.25 CAN.	☐
HAR#16673	ONE HOT COWBOY	$3.75 U.S.	☐
	by Cathy Gillen Thacker	$4.25 CAN.	☐
HH#28952	JADE	$4.99 U.S.	☐
	by Ruth Langan	$5.50 CAN.	☐
LL#44005	STUCK WITH YOU	$3.50 U.S.	☐
	by Vicki Lewis Thompson	$3.99 CAN.	☐

(limited quantities available on certain titles)

AMOUNT	$ _____
POSTAGE & HANDLING	$ _____
($1.00 for one book, 50¢ for each additional)	
APPLICABLE TAXES*	$ _____
TOTAL PAYABLE	$ _____
(check or money order—please do not send cash)	

To order, complete this form and send it, along with a check or money order for the total above, payable to Harlequin Books, to: **In the U.S.:** 3010 Walden Avenue, P.O. Box 9047, Buffalo, NY 14269-9047; **In Canada:** P.O. Box 613, Fort Erie, Ontario, L2A 5X3.

Name: _____

Address: _____ City: _____

State/Prov.: _____ Zip/Postal Code: _____

Account Number (if applicable): _____

*New York residents remit applicable sales taxes.
Canadian residents remit applicable GST and provincial taxes.

Look us up on-line at: http://www.romance.net

HBLAJ98

LOVE & LAUGH

INTO JUNE!

#45 TOO STUBBORN TO MARRY
Marriage Makers, Book II
Cathie Linz

Three bumbling, fumbling fairy godmothers determine that it's time for Deputy U.S. Marshal Ryan Knight to wed! The only problem is he'd already met Miss Right and had just been too stubborn to marry. Now the busy matchmakers fix it so that Courtney Delaney—the woman who stole Ryan's heart—is his next assignment....

#46 HOW THE WEST WAS WED
Jule McBride

Sweet-talkin', sweet-kissin' Jackson West has quite a way with the ladies—and a reputation to uphold. So when the sexy cowboy wagers he can seduce Purity, Miracle Mountain's newest celebrity, he quickly learns he's stepped in it. Because the only way into the lady's life is for Jackson to dress up as "Mrs. Simpson," Purity's housekeeper!

Chuckles available now:

#43 THERE GOES THE BRIDE
Renee Roszel

#44 THE GREAT ESCAPE
Cheryl Anne Porter

LOVE & LAUGHTER™